# MIRROR ISLAND

# MIRROR ISLAND

## Justin Sexton

Above the Rain Collective

2024

Above the Rain Collective
abovetheraincollective@gmail.com
North Georgia, USA

Contributing Editor:  J.A. Sexton

ISBN: 979-8-9899186-2-1

Cover and Interior formatting by J.A. Sexton
Above the Rain logo artwork by Bee Freitag
Cover art: Justin Sexton

TO ALL THE '90s KIDS

# PROLOGUE

Mirror Island pillared out of the Pacific Ocean like a craggy megalith erected by some great, ancient civilization long ago. It was uninhabited, only a mile long, covering about a hundred square acres. Its landscapes were rough and jagged. Fir trees and lush evergreens decorated the rugged terrain and rocky outcroppings adorned its shabby shoreline. The island was situated just off the coast of Washington state and was often caught between an endless blanket of dense fog and heavy clouds. They hung like foreboding ghosts, quilting the etched wilderness, jetting from the frigid water below.

Mirror Island was majestic, yet haunting, much like the trees themselves. Sawtooth bluffs loomed the fringes of the dense taiga. Rigid hillsides and cone-covered forest floors drenched the island year-round. It was overwhelmingly beautiful, a haven for the people on the nearby mainland. Despite all its charm and natural majesty, a dark cloak hung over it. A silent quilt whose threads lay entangled in its heavily frayed and complex past.

In the early 1800s people were banished to Mirror Island and abandoned without food, shelter, tools, or a way out. Legends said many bones were scattered throughout the heavy evergreen thicket. One young boy, however, went alone and never returned. His body was never found. Stories said he fell into a sinkhole and spent weeks alone, slowly withering away.

In April of 1978, a young man named Lewis Ford, a senior from a nearby high school on the mainland went to Mirror Island during spring break to escape his abusive father. A small rowboat he used to travel to the island was discovered on the beach. His backpack and bloody clothing were located dangling from a branch in the forest. Lewis's mother recently passed away and he was an only child left to suffer alone with his violent, alcoholic father.

Some believe he took his own life the night he disappeared, while many others think he fell down one of the steep ravines trying to seek shelter, where he eventually died of starvation. Most folks, however, felt he went to the island for solitude and simply succumbed to the harsh weather. Many people and local search and rescue crews scoured every inch of Mirror Island hoping to find the young student, but all searches over six months led to nothing but the pack and clothing.

Over the past two decades, students from nearby high schools and universities traveled to Mirror Island in honor of Lewis, but also in search of some sort of clue that might shed light on his disappearance or the location of his corpse. Some even said he faked his death and had been living in secrecy on the island for years. The weather there could be severe, especially in the winter. The odds of him surviving were incredibly slim but plausible.

Young kids would push all their fear and anxiety surrounding Lewis' story aside each year and venture out to Mirror Island, wanting to see him lurking in the shadows of the forest. Year after year, they'd migrate to the majestic pillar of rock and evergreen, hoping to solve the mystery of Lewis Ford.

That spring would certainly be no different. It was April 1998 and the twentieth anniversary of Lewis's disappearance was fast approaching. Five high school seniors set to graduate in June made the collective decision to go to Mirror Island and honor the memory of Lewis on the twentieth anniversary of his disappearance.

Unfortunately, not all of them would make it out alive.

# CHAPTER ONE

The headlights of the cranberry-colored minivan flickered off the endless evergreen trees surrounding the dark rural road. The fog was thick and murky, giving an eerie presence to the obsidian night sky overhead. It was hard to see and Spencer struggled to navigate his mother's Nissan Quest through the dense haze. He focused his gaze on the road.

"Everyone shut up for a second. I can't concentrate or see shit. This fog is so heavy," he ordered as he reached for the volume knob on the cd player, turning down the blaring rock music. A thunk sounded on the outside of the van.

"What was that? I think you just hit something?" Alana shouted as she turned her head to look back through the rear windshield.

"It looked like a large fox or a dog," Derek replied with anxiety. He shot up from the captain's seat and glanced out the window.

"Damn it, Spence, you hit an animal!" Chelsea, his bleach blonde, curly-haired girlfriend riding shotgun, yelled.

Alana leaned forward from the very back of the van. Her straight, jet-black hair cascaded over her petite shoulders as she hollered toward the front of the vehicle.

"I saw brown or black fur, it was hard to tell in this fog, but I saw its fur."

"Should we stop and see?" Brandon asked as he licked the paper of the joint he was rolling and put it to his thin, chapped lips.

"No, we're not stopping. Who gives a shit about a stupid fox? We're almost there," Spencer replied as he kept his hands clenched on the steering wheel and snaked the car down the secluded mountain road.

"Don't light that shit yet, Bacon," Chelsea insisted, looking back at Brandon, who was about to spark the lighter. His name was Brandon but everyone called him by his last name... Bacon. Since he smoked so much pot, it was fitting. He had long, flowing brown hair down to his waist and always wore a rock band t-shirt.

Bacon sat in the captain's chair behind his buddy Spencer, who he'd known since preschool. Spencer ran his fingers through his shaggy, dirty blonde hair, feeling annoyed by his boisterous friends creating a ruckus behind him as he tried to focus. He bit the ends of his fingernails and tapped his foot with extreme agitation.

"Wait until we're at the cabin, we're almost there. Just a few minutes, your stoner ass can wait. I don't want to get pulled over a few miles from our destination with all this booze and weed, God knows what else you got on you, Bacon," he stated firmly.

"Well, turn the fucking music back up then. Fuck," Bacon replied as he brushed the strands of hair out of his tan, gaunt face.

"Can we change the music? I'm sick of this chill shit. Let's rip something heavy and sinister," Derek demanded while reaching to the front seat past Spencer and Chelsea to hit the eject button on the CD player. Derek fiddled with the black nylon case in his lap and sifted through his music collection. He scoured through the discs, looking for the right tunes.

"Here, put this mix I made on. It's got Incubus, Korn, Sublime, Soulfly, Tool, and some Deftones on there," Derek pointed out while scratching the top of his newly buzzed and freshly bleached hair.

Metal music ripped through the van speakers. The distortion was thick and murky like the fog hanging ahead.

"Oh shit, we got a flat," Spencer said with a heavy tone of frustration. He eased the van over on the side of the deserted street. It was dark and cloudy, the road ominous and threatening.

"I gotta take a piss, anyway," Bacon replied while sliding the door open and stepping into the wilderness.

The sounds of insects and frogs echoed through the forest. Spencer made his way out of the vehicle and meandered toward the rear.

"I have *Fixaflat* in the back. We can use that to get us to the cabin, then I'll change to the spare in the morning. No sense sitting out here in the dark when we're two miles from the house," he suggested while removing the cap from the canister.

"Sounds good, I wanna get to the cabin ASAP. I'm beginning to think that Jenna was right. Maybe this is a bad omen. We just killed a fox or a dog or some shit, now a flat!" Alana exclaimed from the back of the Nissan.

Their friend Jenna was supposed to make the trip, but she had a premonition shortly after leaving Tacoma. Spencer dropped her off at the mall on the outskirts of town and she called her dad to pick her up. The group pleaded with her to go with them but she insisted she had a bad feeling and would be better off rummaging through band clothes at Hot Topic for an hour, or so, than to risk whatever evil she said was lurking ahead on their trip.

Derek was especially pissed as he was hoping to develop a connection with her during their spring break adventure. Spencer and Chelsea had been together since middle school but everyone else was single. Derek made it clear to his friends that he was after Jenna. They'd all been close since elementary school, some since preschool. Their circle didn't extend much further than the six of them; five now that Jenna had bailed on the trip.

Alana was a bit irritated as well. She, Chelsea, and Jenna talked about this trip since they were in the fourth grade. She knew Chelsea would be too preoccupied with Spencer to give her any attention, so now she knew she would be left alone with Derek and Bacon.

"*FixaFlat's* in, let's go!" Spencer shouted as he jumped in the car and turned the keys in the ignition.

"Do you hear that?" Alana asked while tying her hair into a carefully crafted ponytail.

"Yeah, it sounds like a man screaming," Chelsea replied.

Tension filled the air.

Spencer revved the engine and yelled, "Let's get out of here it's getting louder and closer!"

They all piled back into the Quest and continued the trek to Spencer's family cabin. The home was situated at the far end of Orcas Island. It'd been in his family for generations. It was a minimal, two-bedroom home with a wood stove and a fireplace. It had one bathroom and a complete but outdated kitchen. The cabin was surrounded by giant firs, winding rivers, and ancient old-growth forests.

The group was eager to spend time alone at the vacation home as Spencer's parents usually never allowed them to use it without parental supervision. But they'd be graduating in a couple of months and the trip was a gift from the parents. It was a chance for them all to hang out before graduation and the chaos of the short-lived summer. By September, they'd all be going to college.

Spencer and Chelsea were going to Washington State. Alana was going to Evergreen State and both Derek and Bacon were planning to attend a local community college in Tacoma. They were working on getting an apartment together. After all, they did everything together. They both even worked at Blockbuster Video where Derek was a shift supervisor and Bacon mostly stocked movies and made horror film recommendations to every customer.

"I rented a bunch of stuff for this week. I got..." Bacon started.

Spencer interrupted immediately. "I hope you got VHS 'cause there isn't a DVD player in the cabin."

"I know, dickhead. I got all the VHS tapes. Snagged a few old horror movies. The Omen, The Shining, and Halloween. Y'all never watch old scary films with me, so I'm forcing you into it this week," Bacon said and snickered at Spencer, who he knew was scared of gory movies. Spencer was the biggest in the group, a bulky, broad-chested, lacrosse player with a wide neck that blended into his shoulders like an NFL linebacker, but he was an absolute wimp when it came to scary movies.

"I hope you brought other films, too, not just horror. Some funny shit?" he asked.

"Of course... weak ass. I brought Liar, Liar just for you. It comes out next week on video, I got first dibs. I brought the Fifth Element as well, for a little sci-fi action," Bacon mentioned calmly.

Spencer responded with a head nod before letting out a giant burp. Derek yelled abruptly, "Rumplestiltskin!" while he punched Spencer in the arm repeatedly. Spencer immediately started rattling off beer names.

"Budweiser, Red Dog, Heinekin, Southpaw, and Miller."

"Cut it out, Derek!" Chelsea spat while turning around to scowl at him.

Spencer whipped the van onto the long narrow driveway that fed down the corridor of conifers. The car jetted down the road at an accelerated speed.

"Did you bring Close Encounters? I've never seen it," Alana requested as she poked her head from the rear of the van. The light from the DVD playing on the small TV screen in front of Derek flickered off her face.

"You know it," Bacon replied with enthusiasm.

"You've never seen it? That's one of our favorites. We have watched that flick every year for Bacon's birthday since we were like eight," Spencer commented.

Bacon fumbled with his lighter, anxious to ignite the fat joint he rolled earlier. He pressed the paper between his lips and shuffled in his seat impatiently.

"Yeah, it's one of my all-time favorites... Spielberg's best," he added with a smirk on his face.

The vehicle maneuvered down the final stretch of the private drive. "We're here!" Spencer shouted.

Everyone cheered as they began to disperse in unison. It was dark and hearty clouds moved swiftly in the night sky, creating a shutter effect with the moonlight. The branches of the few deciduous trees creaked in the evening breeze. Off in the holler, an owl echoed through the cool night air. The hoots were sequential, yet inconsistent. Alana panned her head around the dense forest surrounding the cabin and smiled as she heard the owl's nightly call.

"I haven't been here before, this is so cool," she noted.

"I love it," Spencer replied as he patted his jeans pockets for the worn cabin keys. The home was a log-style ranch, built by Spencer's great-great-grandfather in 1920.

"It's my favorite place on Earth," Bacon muttered under his breath as he admired the trees and lit the joint he'd been desperately wanting to smoke since they left Tacoma.

"Yeah, you just like coming up here and getting stoned," Derek proclaimed with a shit-eating grin. Bacon shoved him in the back playfully in response and the two laughed hysterically.

"Fuck, yeah, I do. Still beautiful here, high or not."

"Guys, shut up. I can't find the damn key," Spencer mumbled in frustration.

"You put it in your flannel pocket," Chelsea directed. Her curly hair reflected off the porch light illuminating the front door. She made a stink face at the cobwebs and spiders riddled in every corner of the entrance.

"Maybe they are up your ass?" Derek said with a snicker.

"Shut up, Derek. You look like a little bitch in those Jncos. You still wearing those?" Spencer told him. He checked his back pocket again and cheered.

"Got them," he said while retrieving the rusty keys from his pants pocket.

"Your mom looked like a little bitch last night when she was..." Derek remarked.

Chelsea interrupted with a soft cough, then chimed in, her eyes reprimanding. "Ew, stop there, Derek. You guys are so nasty, is that how you behave when Alana and I aren't around?"

"It's worse, trust me," Bacon admitted proudly.

The glow from the porch light refracted off the chrome balls on his studded metal necklace and created a shimmer. The teens huddled by the front door desperately waiting for Spencer to open it.

"This fucker always jams!" he griped as he lunged toward the entrance. "We're in!" he exclaimed when the door finally budged and he catapulted through the threshold.

Everyone piled in behind him, ready to begin their adventure.

# CHAPTER TWO

"**S**mells musty and dank," Chelsea said, walking into the dimly lit living room. Spencer reached for an antique lamp to reveal the worn and wooden walls.

"Musty and dank. Right up your alley then, Bacon," he replied with a chuckle.

Everyone in the group laughed.

"I'm getting the beer from the car!" Derek exclaimed as he dropped his duffel bag on the dusty cabin floor before running back toward the Quest. The sound of his chain wallet swaying created a rhythmic syncopation with each stride.

Spencer got ahold of a fake ID and managed to buy a van full of booze for the week from a small liquor store outside of town. He was the only one who resembled an adult. He had a full beard and most thought he was in college. Derek and Bacon couldn't even grow one hair on their baby faces.

Derek grabbed a case of lager and a six-pack of Newcastle to share with Bacon. Walking back to the home, a rustle in the bushes caught his attention. He looked to see the faint outline of a fox darting into the shadows.

"I just saw a fox," he said as he entered the home and placed the beer on the outdated kitchen counter.

"I don't want beer, can you grab the tequila?" Chelsea asked with a smug look on her face. Her pointy chin extended in disgust as she rolled her eyes.

"No tequila tonight, let's save that for tomorrow. I don't need you getting alcohol poisoning tonight, Chelsea," Spencer countered with a sneer.

"Beer is gross. Do we have rum?" she spat back, not willing to acquiesce.

"Yeah, one bottle," Derek replied reluctantly.

"I'll have a rum and coke. Spencer, can you make it for me, please?" she asked, kissing him.

"Sure, I will," he mumbled back. "Do you want a rum and coke, too, Alana?"

Alana was touring the cabin, examining all the Pacific Northwest Haida art throughout.

"Sure, but make it a rum and Surge," she replied.

"They call that the Caribbean Shock in Jamaica, 'cause you're shocked when your shit turns green," Bacon chimed in with a wide smile. Derek and Spencer chuckled.

"No, they don't, no they don't at all," Alana interjected while adjusting the filigree-laced choker delicately wrapped around her slender, dark neck. Bacon passed the joint he was hoarding over to Derek, who puffed it a few times before handing it to Spencer. Giant clouds accumulated and created a light haze in the shabby living room. Spencer took a big long drag and coughed excessively.

"Either of you two ladies wanna hit this shit?" he suggested while choking.

"I will," Alana answered.

"Fuck it, I'll take a couple of hits," Chelsea agreed.

Alana nursed it for a moment before she passed it to Chelsea. The smoke began to bellow through the entire room. After she took a few drags and hacked aggressively, Chelsea handed it back to Bacon, who was waiting impatiently for his turn. He grasped it in his clasp like a ruby as he puffed.

"You alright?" Derek asked her while patting her on the back.

Chelsea continued to cough uncontrollably. "Woah," she muttered.

"That's that good Afghan shit!" Bacon yelled a little too loudly.

They finished the joint and the girls sipped their rum and sodas while the boys drank Newcastle and lager.

"It's a bummer Jenna wussed out," Derek grumbled, tipping back his empty beer bottle.

"You were just hoping to get some," Alana said, her voice dripping with sarcasm. Her brown eyes focused on Derek's smug reaction.

"Fuck you!" he shouted back at her.

"She's always got some excuse why she can't join us it seems," Bacon agreed, peeling the label off the glass bottle. He examined the ceiling fan and the dust collecting on the blades.

Spencer searched for the TV remote and responded abruptly, "Her and her premonitions."

Chelsea nodded. "She once made her dad come pick her up at a birthday party because she thought the house was going to burn down that night. It didn't. I love her, but she's crazy."

"She's not crazy, she's just unique," Alana uttered while running her delicate fingers through her hair.

"We get it, Alana, she's your best friend," Derek replied snidely.

"She is and she's been through a lot with her mom dying and all. Cut her some slack. She's freaking nice to all of you."

"I'm just kidding, Alana. Holy shit. Take a chill pill. I feel bad for her after losing her mother like that," Derek answered.

Jenna's mother overdosed on drugs when they were nine years old. It was incredibly hard on her. After her mother's death, Jenna began having visions of the future. She begged and pleaded with everyone to stay in Tacoma, but they refused to hear it. Derek even called her "witch bitch" when she was getting out of the car.

"Speaking of everyone dying, y'all want to watch a scary movie?" Bacon asked the group as he wandered through the kitchen to the old TV and VHS player. The cabin floorboards creaked with each step he took.

"Let's do something lighter tonight. It's been a long day," Spencer commented while putting his arm around Chelsea.

"Scared already!" Bacon declared with assurance.

Chelsea smiled as she shifted her bleach-blonde hair out of her freckled face and kissed Spencer on the cheek. "I love my big scaredy cat."

"I love you, too," Spencer whispered in her ear.

"Gross," Derek groaned in disgust.

"I'm grabbing another beer," Brandon announced while opening the fridge and reaching for a Newcastle.

"Don't drink too many too fast tonight, Bacon. I don't need you pissing on my grandma's antique couch!" Spencer insisted with irritation.

"I can't make any promises," Bacon replied with a jovial cackle. He cracked another brew and clanked it against Derek's in celebration.

Midnight approached and the gang found themselves extremely exhausted. They decided to go to sleep after midnight as they had a big week planned. Tomorrow they'd hang out at the cabin during the day and parade around the beach. Then later that night, they planned to watch old horror films. Everyone dispersed to their sleeping arrangements. The cabin was quiet while the high school seniors slept peacefully.

Nighttime passed with the rising of the sun. Rays of daylight streamed through the old windows. It was a beautiful Sunday morning and they were looking forward to a day of venturing around the Pacific coast. The afternoon came and went, before they knew it they were back from their afternoon stroll at the beach. The sun was beginning to set as rain clouds rolled in.

"Damn, it's really pouring out there," Alana said.

Bacon rose from the couch and hovered over the tacky Magnavox television trapped between layers of heavily lacquered wood. "What do you wanna watch first?" he asked as he shuffled through the plastic Blockbuster cases.

"What are our options?" Derek asked.

"The Omen, Halloween. Oh, I forgot I brought Scream, Scream 2, and I Know What You Did Last Summer," Bacon replied with his eyes fixated on each case.

"Anything but I Know What You Did Last Summer!" Derek chimed in swiftly.

"The Omen. It's something I have never seen," Chelsea noted with hesitation.

"You're kidding! The Omen it is. Works for me!" Bacon exclaimed in agreement. He pulled the tape from its clear rental container and placed it into the receiver. The tape fed into the machine quickly, and the noise of mechanical movement shifting in the player was repetitive and rhythmic.

"Have you seen this, Alana?" Bacon asked.

"I have. It's been a while, but I saw it when I was like twelve at Jenna's house. Her dad rented it and watched it with us. We were so scared, none of us slept that night. I had nightmares for weeks. I haven't seen it since, though," she answered, lost in the memory.

Bacon reached for the bulky remote control and turned the volume up as loud as it would go.

"Not so loud!" Spencer commanded from the couch.

"Relax, it's an old-ass movie," Bacon commented back, reaching for a Surge cola and a slice of Tombstone pepperoni pizza. He held the bright green aluminum can in his hands and examined the red splatter and bold black text.

"Man, I love me some Surge!"

# CHAPTER THREE

The Omen ended and they decided to take a smoke break outside. The rain was still falling, so the teens went onto the screened-in back porch to puff cigarettes and cannabis.

"That movie scares the shit out of me every time," Spencer said awkwardly. His eyes were low and soft as he spoke.

"Every horror movie scares the shit out of you. You thought the Puppetmasters was freaky," Bacon teased.

"Fuck that shit! The Puppetmasters is scary as hell, no doubt!" Derek protested.

"The Omen's not even that terrifying. I was so scared of that film growing up, but these days it just makes me laugh. It was all for you, Damian. Then the bitch jumps out the window. Shit's hilarious," Bacon responded while rolling up a blunt with a Camel cigarette pressed in his mouth.

"What do you guys wanna watch next?" Chelsea asked.

"Halloween! I wanna see some seventies titties," Derek shouted with a chuckle.

"That's the only way you are seeing any action tonight," Alana pointed out.

They all laughed and went back inside to get a drink except Bacon and Derek, who both stayed to finish the blunt. They passed it back and forth quietly.

"I'm high as fuck," Derek mumbled.

Bacon stood up from his seat as lightning flashed and illuminated the surrounding forest. The woodline turned from black to blue in an instant. "Me too, let's go inside... Holy shit! Did you see that?" Bacon exclaimed in confusion.

"See what?" Derek asked.

"I swear I just saw a man in the woods," he answered, his eyes like saucers.

"Quit fucking with me, let's go watch the movie."

"I'm not messing around. I saw an old man with a bushy, black beard in a dark green raincoat. I could see him pull the hood over his gnarly head. He was just standing there like a giant turd in the yard," Bacon voiced with extreme concern.

"Hey, fucker!" Derek shouted toward the saturated surrounding greenwood.

Bacon joined in. "Hey, old man!"

"Yo, fucker!" Derek yelled at the top of his lungs as Spencer came running out on the porch in a panic.

"What the hell are you yelling at?" he asked.

"I saw an old guy with a beard, standing in the fucking rain like a creepo staring at us," Bacon told him.

"It's probably just old man Sinclair. He lives next door. Tall, skinny, guy with a big, gray beard. He's harmless, stop shouting at him. He'll tell my parents," Spencer warned.

"Isn't he like eighty? This guy didn't look that old," Bacon said.

"Well, he's a weirdo hanging out in the rain like that at ten o'clock at night," Derek mentioned, taking a giant swig of his lukewarm beer.

"He's old as fucking dirt, probably has dementia or some shit," Spencer explained as he motioned them inside. He continued as he turned the porch light off.

"Come watch the movie, guys," he insisted.

"Hold your horses, we're coming," Bacon grumbled. The dank smell of sweet petrichor permeated the cold, wet Pacific air.

"Don't tell the girls you saw old man Sinclair lurking in the rain. It'll scare them. I don't need Chelsea being freaked out all night, especially now that we're watching the OG Halloween," Spencer whispered to Derek and Brandon.

"Of course, man," both boys said in agreement.

The second movie wrapped up just after midnight. The rain continued to plummet for hours. It was a fitting backdrop for the slew of horror films the group devoured like old Halloween candy. Everyone reverted to being silly while playing a drinking game. The friends were in good spirits and enjoying their time together. It was a long senior year and they all looked forward to graduation. For now, however, they were enjoying one another's company as they tried to digest every bit of it they could.

Spencer was preparing to leave for a summer job working for his uncle, and Bacon always visited his family farm in Oregon for half the summer, so for the boys especially, this was one final hurrah before completing high school.

Spencer would be heading out to California the day after graduation, so they soaked up every moment together. *Halloween* ended and Spencer took Chelsea to the bathroom to help her as she threw up before carrying her to the bedroom to sleep it off. Derek and Bacon went out front to smoke cigarettes and look at the trees while Alana retired to her room.

"Let me get a smoke, B," Derek said while making a scissor motion with his index and middle finger.

"Are you out already?" Bacon replied.

Derek pulled the hood of his raincoat over his cleanly buzzed head. He was tall and lanky, his scalp almost touched the tall fir branches above them while they puffed cigarettes under the canopy. "No, I left mine inside," he replied, agitated.

"Here you go. You owe me one, those are Turkish golds, too. Remember that shit."

"Chill. I know," Derek responded. The front door flung open suddenly.

"Look who it is. She passed out?" Bacon asked Spencer as he walked out the front door.

"Oh, yeah, she's hammered. She'll be fine in the morning, though," Spencer replied, taking a drag of his Newport. He blew several smoke rings into the night sky and admired the constellations.

"Why do you give her so many weed hits when you know it makes her spin?" Derek inquired.

"So she'd pass out sooner and we can hang out," Spencer admitted, sheepishly.

"That's such a dick move, dude," Bacon said with a sneer. He adjusted his red beanie, removed his black Airwalks, and shook the forest debris from the insides before putting them back on.

"Whatever. When do you guys wanna head out to Mirror Island tomorrow? Are you both still down for two nights?" Spencer asked reluctantly. He never liked camping.

"Hell yeah!" they both replied simultaneously.

"Early the better," Derek responded, noticing something moving in the shadows by the underbrush.

"Y'all hear that?" Bacon inquired with a whisper.

"Probably a fox or old man Sinclair's dog, Rudy," Spencer slurred. He swayed side to side like a giant sunflower in a heavy breeze during peak summer.

"Probably Bigfoot," Derek joked.

"Maybe it's your mom, Derek! She's emerging from some small hairy crevice coming to bitch at you with her nasty ass snaggletooth for smoking dope in the woods like a degenerate. Derek! Derek, it's your fat ass mother!" Bacon said with a giggle. Brandon continued his imitation of Derek's mom. He was now stomping on the ground with his hands out away from him as if to hold some gelatinous fat-like substance that was spilling out from his slender frame.

"Derek, Derek," both Spencer and Bacon began to chant. They were incredibly amused, however, Derek was not. He got red and embarrassed. He shouted something in Spanish and smacked them both in the face.

"Yeah, well, my mom's not a slut like your drunk ass mom," Derek spat, kicking his feet toward Brandon.

"I'd totally bang your mom, Bacon. All day, every day," Spencer joked, humping the air.

"Join the club," Derek cheered in agreement.

"Fuck you both!" Bacon voiced in anger. He always became immediately defensive when they talked about having sex with his mother. He was often aloof but perverse comments about his mom bothered him immensely. He heard it all the time and he was a momma's boy through and through.

"Y'all are crass," Alana said, walking outside with disgust hanging from her chiseled face.

"Alana!" all three boys shouted.

"Can't sleep?" Spencer asked.

"Well, it is hard to when you three are so fucking loud," she noted in a whisper with a shiver.

"Get a jacket, a smoke, and join us," Derek suggested.

"Ok," she replied, heading back inside for her Nautica fleece, Marlboro 100s, and purple toboggan.

"Are you excited for Mirror Island tomorrow?" Bacon asked her. His eyes fixated on Alana's eyes. He admired the way they resembled the color of newly produced pinecones in the spring.

Mirror Island was riddled with them in late April and Alana hoped to collect a few to draw for her final high school art project. She put on her jacket and lit her cig.

The flick of her zippo was nostalgic and reminiscent of a time when the crew were freshmen. Bacon gave the lighter to

Alana for her fifteenth birthday when they were hanging out at the skate park.

"Of course. I've been wanting to go since I was nine. I'm so excited."

"Nice. Still got the old zippo, I see. That's rad," Bacon observed with glee.

"Of course," Alana said, then let out a big yawn.

"You bring any drugs, B?" Spencer voiced oddly as he staggered around the porch like a walrus.

"You know it! I got some ecstasy for all of us for Mirror Island and some acid for us to take when we go to Spirit Falls later in the week."

"Dude! Yes!" Derek yelled with his hands over his head.

"Sounds like fun. I'm game for rolling on the island," Alana replied. She was apprehensive as the drug was new to her, but she was interested in broadening her horizons like the rest of the group.

"It's going to be so cool, man," Bacon said exuberantly.

"You get it all from your sister?" Derek asked.

"Yeah, Kare came through, as always," he replied. Bacon's sister Kara was a sophomore at Evergreen State and often came home with plenty of illegal treats for her brother and his friends.

"I say we head out to the island around noon," Spencer suggested as he rubbed his tired eyes.

"Works for me," Derek agreed, flicking his cigarette butt into an abandoned concrete planter on the porch.

"Me too," Alana and Bacon both muttered.

"Alana, why are you so much cooler than all the other girls? Sorry, Spence," Derek asked abruptly.

"Cause I'm not into drama. I have nothing to prove to anyone."

"I dig it," Bacon responded, zipping up his North Face jacket. The motion covered the *Dark Side of the Moon* artwork on his faded black tee shirt buried beneath his worn flannel.

"Oh, Chelsea is a fucking drama queen. I love her, but she ain't right," Spencer said with a slur.

"You need to go to bed, man, you're fucking drunk," Derek suggested. Spencer stumbled as he towered over them like the giant evergreens they were huddled under.

"We all need to go to bed. It's one. I'm crashing out," Alana agreed as she put her cigarette out and went inside.

"I'm with her, good night, guys," Spencer mumbled.

"Goodnight," Bacon and Derek whispered. For a moment it was just the two of them outside, listening to the rustling of the wind in the pine needles.

"You got money saved for rent in August when we get a place?" Derek asked.

"Yeah, I got five hundred right now."

"You need more than that, man."

"Well, no one is covering this weed everyone's smoking on and the LSD and the rolls I got," Bacon responded with irritation.

"True, true. Here's forty, man," Derek said as he reached into his back pocket and retrieved his chain wallet. He pulled out two crisp twenty-dollar bills and handed them to Bacon.

"Shit. Thanks, bud."

"I can't wait to get our place, we're gonna get so fucked up and skate so much. I love coming out here but there is nowhere to shred."

"I know, I'd love to get some skating in," Bacon agreed as he tossed his cigarette butt. "Anyway, I'm crashing. Goodnight."

"Goodnight, man,"

\*\*\*

The clouds rolled out early the next morning. By sunrise, the sky was clear and blue. The group got up, ate breakfast, and headed to the beach until afternoon when they loaded up for their ride to Mirror Island. Once they were packed up and ready to camp, they made their way across the Pacific which took about half an hour. Spencer maneuvered the bay boat around the entire outline before mooring at a dock on the backside of the island.

"Looks like nobody's here right now. May just be us on the island tonight." He examined the deserted landscape. Dark clouds fluttered in the heavens, they were all-seeing and foreboding as they passed over the lush landscape.

"Sweet, we can be loud and party tonight!" Derek proclaimed. He clenched a Southpaw beer bottle in his grasp.

"It's bigger than I thought it would be," Alana stated as she observed the towering conifers that extended from the rocky outcroppings.

"It's beautiful," Chelsea whispered in Spencer's ear.

"Have you never been here, Spence?" Bacon inquired, his eyes panned the beach as Spencer cut the engine off.

"I've been past it on the boat many times, but I have yet to step foot on the island itself," he admitted.

"Well, let's do the damn thing," Bacon hollered toward the sky.

"There is something spooky and ominous about it," Spencer said, peering at the contoured cliffs.

# CHAPTER FOUR

T he group scattered about in search of a good camping spot close to the boat. They worked together to erect the six-person tent, gather the sleeping bags, and sort the necessary cooking supplies. After an hour of unpacking and setting up, everyone was on the shoreline hanging out and mostly doing their own thing.

Spencer and Chelsea took a walk while Bacon and Derek tossed a frisbee on the sand. Alana took some time to be alone and draw in her sketchpad. She was recently awarded an art scholarship to Evergreen State and looked forward to starting college in the fall.

She was patient as she took her time drawing the rugged terrain and serrated outcroppings that decorated the circumference of her peripheral. As she sketched the shape of the rock faces and the silhouettes of the fir trees, she couldn't help but let her mind wander. She'd waited almost ten years to make this journey to Mirror Island and here she was. A feeling of disappointment washed over her as she thought about how Jenna wasn't there with her. A part of Alana couldn't help but think maybe Jenna was right, that her feeling held some validity, but she shoved the thought aside and continued shading in her drawing.

Chelsea and Spencer meandered through the lush, temperate forests. The sun peeked through the clouds and projected a sunbeam between the green foliage onto their young faces. The couple stepped into a dense forest thicket, far away from the beaten path. As they trudged through the woods, branches and natural debris crunched beneath their feet.

"That's disturbing," Spencer mumbled under his breath.

"What? Oh, that is bizarre, is that a painted baby doll's head on a stake?" Chelsea replied with her hand over her mouth.

Spencer reached back for his girlfriend and held her hand in his firm grasp as they ventured further into the wilderness. "Look, there's more of them. One, two, three, four, five, six, seven, eight, nine!"

"Maybe we should turn around?" Chelsea suggested.

"They're everywhere around here... creepy," Spencer replied in horror.

They shifted further into the dense overgrowth and approached a small meadow with vibrant ferns and forest flora. Nestled throughout the ever-unfolding beauty were several tall wooden spears with various-sized plastic babydoll heads and body parts attached to them. The heads were painted to look demonic and evil with black and red paint. It seemed as if someone decorated each severed head to look intentionally demented and wicked.

"They look like they have blood on them, that's fucking strange," Spencer whispered.

He wasn't wrong. Each head and extremities were painted with what appeared to be dried blood. Black ink filled in all of the eyeballs and some of the heads had homemade horns and antlers fastened to them. Various peach-colored, plastic skulls with *666* written on their foreheads and tiny pentagrams etched into their third eye were strategically placed around the woods.

"I don't like this, Spencer. Let's turn around, please!" Chelsea demanded as she tugged on her boyfriend's fleece jacket. Raindrops trickled off the damp evergreen needles, enriching the organic landscapes surrounding the odd scenery before them.

Spencer continued to tug Chelsea further toward the display. He carefully examined the stakes, which resembled spears. Each one stood about five feet high. They were wooden and appeared hand-carved. Some had plastic arms and legs sticking out of the sides, while others protruded through heads perched on top.

"These back here look to have animal bones and antlers attached. It seems like some kind of satanic altar. This is so fucking weird," Spencer muttered uncomfortably.

"Let's go back, now. Spencer, please."

"Chelsea, no one is here, we're the only ones on the island. Look, it goes even further back, easily another two hundred feet. Spencer gazed down what looked like a worn path lined by even more spears with baby doll heads and animal bones adorning them. The tiny plastic hands held small, intricately crafted metal trinkets. As he drifted further down the faint trail, he was met by a shrine of animal skulls and mangled bones. Some were enormous rib cages, while others were smaller and neatly stacked on top of giant deer skulls.

"What the fuck? What kind of animal bones are these?" Spencer asked.

"It appears like a collage of many different kinds. That looks like a sea lion rib cage and skull, that's an elk skull, that's a walrus skeleton. This is morbid. I'm turning around and going back," Chelsea insisted. She ran as fast as she could to the beach. When she reached the shore, she was screaming frantically.

"We just found some scary shit. I'm really freaked out!" she shouted toward her friends at the shoreline.

"Woah, calm down. What happened? Where's Spencer?" Alana asked, lifting her head from her sketchpad in a panic.

"He's way back in the woods, he wouldn't leave. He's in a trance or something," Chelsea replied.

"Leave what?" Derek asked.

"This creepy shrine of painted baby doll heads, and body parts with animal skulls. It's satanic and demonic. I think we should leave," she said with an intense quiver.

"That sounds cool as fuck, show me!" Bacon declared.

"It's not cool, Brandon, and I don't know where Spencer is. He's back there somewhere," she insisted.

"Well, you have to show us to find him," Derek stated with a smile.

"I'm not going back there," Chelsea retorted.

Just then, Spencer emerged from the forest onto the beach.

"Spencer!" Chelsea cried out. She ran over and put her arms around his burly chest.

"I wanna see the creepy altar! Spencer, you gotta show us!" Bacon exclaimed.

"I'll show you guys, follow me."

The trio traversed their way through the greenwood. As they approached the chantry, Bacon let out a roar of excitement.

"This is awesome!"

"It's spooky, but it's so fucking cool. Who do you think made it? Lewis Ford?" Derek asked.

"Lewis Ford is dead as hell, man. Probably some weirdo locals to Orcas Island coming out and making bizarre shit to scare folks out here," Spencer said.

"This is so grotesque," Derek mumbled.

The boys ventured back to the shore and found Alana and Chelsea talking quietly.

"She's freaked out by the shrine and wants to leave," Alana told them.

"You gotta come see it, Alana, it's so fucking sweet!" Bacon begged.

"Come with us, we'll show you," Derek said.

"I can't be the only one who hasn't seen it, show me."

Derek and Bacon lead Alana to the altar while Spencer and Chelsea waited on the beach. When they returned, the couple was nowhere to be seen.

"Where the fuck did they go?" Derek asked.

"Probably back to the boat," Alana responded.

Bacon threw his arms in the air in distress. "Great, I bet they wanna leave now. Fucking Chelsea. She ruins everything."

"I don't see them on the boat," Derek commented as he glanced over to the deserted vessel.

"They probably went to fuck, then," Bacon grumbled.

"He's probably right," Alana agreed.

Spencer convinced Chelsea in her vulnerable state to follow him around the backside of a nook near the inlet of the island. They were kissing and undressing when a shuffle at the far edge of the woodline caught their attention. Dusk was approaching and the sun was slowly descending.

"Stop, Spencer. I heard something."

"It's probably only a small woodland creature," he whispered as he continued to kiss her.

"Spencer, stop! I said stop!"

Chelsea got up and slipped her bra on. Spencer darted toward the shadows, which were increasing in size as darkness slowly dissipated out amongst the wilderness. Spencer stomped and paraded around the base of several fir trees.

"Rawrrrr!!" he screamed at the top of his lungs as he shifted out of Chelsea's sight.

"Get back over here!" she yelled, putting her sweater on. She hurried to gather her pants, shoes, and jacket.

"Stop fucking off, let's go back to the group," she shouted off into the blackness. She waited for a response but heard nothing. It was unnaturally quiet, even the animals had fallen silent. Chelsea rubbed the goosebumps forming on her arms, sensing she wasn't alone.

"Spencer! Stop messing around. It's not funny. I don't like when you mess with me in the woods." Again she paused and listened for him.

Chelsea stepped into the shadows and waited patiently for him to come to his senses. All of a sudden, she screamed in horror as she felt something thin pull tightly around her neck. It was sharp and cut through her skin. Her blood oozed down her throat toward her chest. She gagged and her mouth gurgled as she spit blood and took her last breaths.

Her body collapsed and toppled on top of her boyfriend's mutilated corpse she hadn't noticed she was standing right over. Spencer was splayed out on the forest floor dead. Blood decorated his neck and multiple treble fish hooks hung from his ears, nose, and neck. His skin was covered in lashes and several deep gashes.

Mirror Island was still. The sky fell dark and the evening breeze was pronounced. A heavy gust ripped through the trees, creating a scuffle in the canopies. The island was eerie beneath the dense celestial life birthing overhead. The scene in the forest was horrid and demonic. Spencer and Chelsea lay dead in pools of blood and forest debris. Their bodies were covered in several conifer limbs and various evergreen branches. Carefully placed on their corpses were severed baby doll heads, a morbid and grisly scene.

The man shuffled off into the darkness to hide amongst the wild.

# CHAPTER FIVE

The stars began to peek out from behind the clouds and the moon ascended alongside Spencer and Chelsea's souls as their spirits left their bodies. Constellations surfaced and the others realized then, their friends were nowhere to be found.

"Where are they? It's been a couple of hours now. They should've been back already. It's getting too dark to see out there," Alana expressed concerned, her voice wavering.

"They're probably going for round three, you know how they are," Bacon snickered.

"Hardly, pun intended," Derek joked.

Bacon laughed hysterically and stomped his feet. "Good one," he chattered.

Alana grew irritated. "Cut it out. I'm not kidding, you guys. I hope they didn't get lost, or worse, ditch us out here."

"Lost? It's a tiny ass island," Derek countered, lighting a smoke.

"Spencer, you bitch, where are you at!" Bacon yelled at the top of his lungs. They all listened for a response, then started calling the couple's names.

"Chelsea! Spencer! Chelsea! Spencer!" they screamed as they hiked along the beach, following the coastline. They maneuvered around several magnificent pieces of driftwood scattered along the shore.

"I don't hear them at all. Jenna was right, this was a bad idea," Alana murmured while she buried her face in her hands in distress. She covered her eyes and fell silent in fear.

"They're fine, we're the only ones on the island," Derek replied, sipping his beer.

"There's not even bears here," Bacon offered as he pulled out a small chillum and a tiny glass jar full of cannabis.

"Are you going to smoke weed right now?" Alana asked, her irritation proliferating by the second.

"Shit's intense. I need to chill. Derek, do you want to hit this?" Bacon inquired while passing the intricately designed glass piece over to Derek.

"Please!" Derek answered, bellowing a cloud of tobacco smoke into the cool night air. They continued walking along the beach when the silhouette of an empty pontoon boat caught their eyes.

"Whose boat is that? That wasn't here earlier when Bacon and I were throwing frisbees," Derek said, fear lingering along each syllable.

"I bet it's only kids from the nearby YMCA. They have a camp across the water off of Orcas Island. The kids like to run away at night and come out here to drink and get stoned," Brandon replied.

"It's true. Both Bacon and I went there when we were in seventh grade," Derek agreed.

The moonlight glistened off the glassy Pacific. The moon's reflection shimmered on the surface like sunlight refracting in a cracked mirror.

"Didn't you both get kicked out of there?" Alana joked.

"Yeah, for smoking dope and hoarding vodka," Bacon replied as he removed his beanie and tied his hair into a ponytail.

"You guys are corrupt," she uttered.

"We know," they said together at once.

Alana observed the dilapidated and rusty pontoon boat. It was old, easily from the seventies. "There's no one around it, though. Those kids wouldn't leave the beach and venture into the woods when it's this dark."

"Not if they want to have a fire," Bacon suggested.

"Yeah, if they build a campfire, they go into the woods. That way the camp counselors can't see them from the other island," Derek replied while scratching his freshly buzzed head. The bit of hair left plastered on his scalp stood up in yellowish spikes.

"I should've worn a hat, it's getting cold," he said.

"You should've worn a hat 'cause you look ridiculous with all that *Sun-in* on your head. Holy shit! Did you use the whole bottle? Your hair is orange as hell. If you'd kept the longer hair, you'd look like that demon elf guy on that weird-ass Christmas movie," Bacon teased.

"The Heat Miser." Alana chuckled.

"Suck it," Derek grumbled, taking swipes at them.

"Anyway. He's right, Alana. The kids like to get fucked up around the fire, it's cold. They don't want to sit by the breezy beach. Let's go look for their campfire and fuck with them. Shit, Spencer and Chelsea probably already did and raided their booze like savages. Maybe that's why they're ignoring us," Bacon stated with certainty.

"I'm game," Derek chimed in.

They patrolled the outskirts of the forests near the shore, searching for signs of life but didn't see anything.

"I don't see a fire, I don't hear anyone. It's dead quiet, guys. Whose fucking boat is that and where are Chelsea and Spencer? This isn't fun anymore," Alana whispered.

"Spencer! Where the hell are you!" Derek proclaimed to the heavens above. Bacon joined in and quickly both boys were howling at the moon.

"Great, draw attention to us. Let whatever psycho might be running loose know exactly where we are," she articulated with aggravation.

"The island is bigger than we realize, Alana, stop stressing," Derek said, his dirty fingers clasping a beer can in his grasp. He cracked the beer and took a giant swig.

"You guys aren't concerned at all that we can't find them and that we aren't alone on the island?" she asked.

"I'm not. Spencer and Chelsea are probably fucking off, absorbing as much alone time as possible. It's spring break. Of course, folks are camping out here!" Bacon exclaimed.

Derek took another gulp of beer. "Hopefully, it's hot chicks and they are looking to party."

"You two are useless," Alana stated, pushing ahead of the boys.

The three teenagers walked to their campsite, hoping to find Chelsea and Spencer when they returned.

Alana sat in the sand and let her hair down. "Guys, this is concerning. It's getting super late," she mumbled.

"Well, maybe we should venture into the woods. The moon is higher in the sky, it's almost full. We got flashlights," Derek said.

"Grab the headlamps," Alana agreed.

"And more booze," Derek shouted, grabbing the tequila bottle and a few beers. He quickly filled a silver flask with the liquor, shoving it and two beers into his jacket pockets. He cracked the beer in his hand and chugged it.

"Take it easy, man, you know how you get. We don't need you putting on an emotional display tonight, screaming shit in Spanish," Bacon told him.

"What are you, my mother? Fuck off," Derek uttered.

"Just don't need you wiggin' out like you did at Billy's party a few weeks ago."

Alana laughed for a moment. "I heard about that. You were fighting trees and yourself in the mirror in the bathroom for like an hour, Spencer said."

"True story," Bacon sang.

"Fuck you both. You can't tell me what to do!" he screamed in their faces before guzzling the rest of the beer. He took the can and crushed it in his hand, throwing it at the orange tent.

"You're not my dad! You can't tell me what to do!" Alana exclaimed while mocking Derek.

She and Bacon both imitated him. The rage began to swell up inside Derek. He was already incredibly insecure, but now he was being mimicked in front of his best friend and a girl he liked. His inner demons grew with each breath he took in fury.

"I hate you both!" he growled in anger. Derek was enraged. He pulled one of the beer cans out of his fleece pocket and stormed off into the night.

"Let him go. He's gone over the edge. He'll blackout soon, then pass out on the beach and sleep it off. It's cool," Bacon told Alana.

"No, it's not cool, Brandon," she replied, annunciating his name.

"Oh, shit is real now. You called me Brandon."

"Not everything is a joke. We have no idea where Spencer and Chelsea are, we don't need to lose Derek, too."

Alana was worried. She knew her concerns were valid. It was well after eleven and midnight was approaching fast. It was clear they weren't alone and Derek's dramatic performance was only making matters worse.

"Yes, ma'am," Bacon answered.

The two continued to traverse the coastline for a while before they rested on a giant piece of driftwood abandoned on the rocky shore. The big dipper hung like a beacon in the midnight sky. Stars twinkled and shimmered as thin clouds passed by overhead. Planets and meteors appeared in the heavens.

Mirror Island stood in the ocean almost like a human skull on the surface, struggling for air. The mood was chaotic as Alana and Bacon discussed what to do.

"Let's just go back to the boat and find them," Alana suggested.

"You're way too worried about this. Derek is fucking wasted and Chelsea and Spencer are fucking or something. Plain and simple. I've seen this story a hundred times. Relax and have fun. It's spring, 1998, bitches!" Bacon howled.

"Are you ever gonna grow up?" Alana asked, her brow arching with concern.

"Not any time soon. Live it up, Alana. We're on Mirror Island. You graduate from high school in a couple of months, you get a full ride to do art and shit, and you're hot. Enjoy it. Maybe come get a little bacon," he offered with a grin.

"Never in a million years, you perv."

"I was kidding," he said, blushing at the sand.

"No, you weren't."

"Yeah, I was. It would be weird, anyway."

"That's for sure. Everything about you is weird."

"Aint that the fucking truth," Bacon joked.

"We gotta find our friends, ASAP," Alana said as she observed the foreboding clouds in the sky.

"Derek is close to passing out, he's too far gone. Trust me, I know that kid's drinking cycles. He went from zero to a hundred and sixty tonight already. He's toasted."

# CHAPTER SIX

Derek was buried inside his head. His thoughts were heavily fermented in alcohol and he was now acting off of emotion.

"Fuck them. They wanna make fun of me? They don't know me. They don't know what I've been through. All the shit with my mom, my douchebag dad. My cousins and family are back in Mexico. They don't know what it's like living with my asshole brother, who beats on me all the time 'cause he thinks he's in a gang," he slurred under his breath.

"So sick of this shit. They aren't my friends, they don't know me," he continued, ranting aggressively.

Derek was struggling deeply. His father recently ran out on his mother. His mom was hooked on pain pills and both of his brothers were, as well. Derek's home life was in ruins and he was alone trying to pick up the debris. With each step he took out of the forest, he staggered and stumbled, spilling tequila from his flask.

He reached the beach and went to sit on the boat alone and wallow in his sorrow. Derek looked up at the stars and tripped when he missed his step onto the boat. He shifted back and forth for a moment and caught his balance before falling again. Just as he was about to hit the ground, someone caught him. He turned around to greet the person.

"Who the fuck are you?" he mumbled incoherently.

The man grabbed Derek and in one motion, wrapped fishing line tightly around the teen's neck. The bearded man pulled firmly. The fishing line began to sink into Derek's skin as blood pooled out. Derek fought to scream but nothing came out. His vocal cords were slit as his body sunk to the deck of the boat, his head barely attached to his body. It was hanging on by a thread of flesh as it swayed in the evening breeze.

Several minutes passed before Alana and Bacon decided to head back to camp. They were expecting to see Derek there drunk and hopefully Spencer and Chelsea had returned, as well. They were both nervous when they returned to camp and were the only ones there. The sound of frogs and crickets serenading the twilight was intoxicating, yet spooky. Fear set in.

"I bet Derek's passed out on the boat," Bacon said as he ran over to the vessel and hopped on the deck. He screamed in horror. "What the fuck, holy shit!"

He began to shake and vomit. Alana came over in a panic. She cried out an unsettling shrill before puking on the deck. The teens tripped over Derek's corpse as they tried to get away from the terrible scene.

"We need to get out of here," Bacon mumbled as he spit bile from his mouth.

Alana searched the inside of the boat and checked the ignition for the keys. "We don't have the keys, Spencer still has them!"

She maneuvered past her friend's mutilated body to get off the boat. Bacon followed her down the dock to the shoreline.

"We have to find Spencer and Chelsea and get out of here!" Bacon cried out.

"They're probably dead, too."

"What do we do, then? Someone or something is hunting us!" Bacon shrieked.

Alana reached for the knife in her pocket before remembering there was a Glock on the bay boat. "Spencer's gun is on board, I'm going back for it," she whispered.

She searched the inside captain's room and located the box the weapon was in. She drew the pistol out and checked the safety. She noticed the box of bullets and grabbed those.

"Got it," she proclaimed as she jumped off the boat and onto the dock. The tattered planks reverberated when her red Converse shoes hit them.

"Let me see it," Bacon insisted as he shifted strands of hair out of his dark eyes.

"Hell no. I know I'm a better shot than you," she shouted back at him.

"Fair enough," he replied.

"We have to find Spencer, dead or alive at this point. We need those keys."

"I'm scared to death, Alana," Bacon said, his body trembling.

"It's only midnight. We have at least five and a half more hours until the sun starts rising. Fuck. Jenna was right, she was right," Alana stated with shame.

"What should we do now?" Bacon asked in horror.

"We need to be on guard until dawn and try to find Spencer and Chelsea. We need the keys to get off this horrible island." Alana began to cry. The fear inside her was immense.

"I gotta go to the tent, I need to see if my phone has service," Bacon said as he quickly shifted off the dock and toward the campsite. Alana followed him over. When they reached the site, it was clear someone had been rummaging through their stuff. Bacon searched the inside of the tent of his pack and took out the small phone.

"Shit, no service," he muttered. He began to weep.

"You thought you'd have cell service out here? We are fucked, Brandon."

# CHAPTER SEVEN

"**O**f course, there's no service out here," Alana complained.

"It was worth a shot, at least," Bacon offered, his voice quaking, despite his assurance.

"You're right," she admitted, wishing they'd never stepped foot on the island. "We had to try."

A mechanical sound close by caught their attention. Alana's ears perked up. "Is that the boat? That sounds like Spencer's engine."

They ran toward the dock to see Spencer's boat taking off across the ocean into the moonlight.

"Spencer's ditching us?" Bacon questioned in shock.

"Use your head, Brandon. With Derek's dead body?" Alana replied in frustration.

"What if he killed Derek?"

"Why would he kill Derek? They're friends," she asked with confusion.

"Senior stress, man. He's been so worried about getting into Washington State. He hasn't got the acceptance letter like Chelsea did. Plus, there was that rumor going around before school let out last week that Chelsea and Derek hooked up at Billy's party."

Bacon wasn't wrong. There certainly had been a rumor that Chelsea had been cheating on Spencer with Derek.

"It isn't true, that rumor is bullshit! I was with her and Spencer the whole night," Alana exclaimed, clenching strands of hair in her nervous grasp.

"Maybe they didn't that night, but I heard through the grapevine that they've been for a year now."

"I don't believe it. Spencer and Chelsea have been together since middle school and he's been obsessed with her since like third grade. No way," she insisted.

"Then why did his boat just take off?" Bacon asked.

"I don't know, but we may be safe for the time being. I have a feeling."

"Why is that?" he asked.

"I think whoever was after us just left. All of a sudden the atmosphere feels lighter. Do you feel that?"

"We're stuck now, how are we going to get out of here?" Bacon questioned in a panic.

"Let's check that pontoon boat for keys," Alana answered, her brown eyes panning the beach.

"Good idea."

She grabbed Bacon by the jacket. "Follow me!" she yelled as she tugged him along the rocky coastline.

When they got to the pontoon boat, they looked for keys but there weren't any.

"Shit, I don't see them," Bacon whined.

"I'm guessing whoever's pontoon boat this is, killed Derek and took off with Spencer's boat. I bet both him and Chelsea are dead. It's now been hours since we've seen or heard from them," Alana expressed, full of fear.

"Our only hope is kids from the camp show up tomorrow, or day hikers even, otherwise we are trapped here," Bacon muttered.

"Let's hope so. Right now we still need to be on edge. Those doll heads and bones are freaking me out more now," she confessed.

"No kidding. What if some crazy man was trapped here and this was his chance out?" he asked. Bacon searched his pockets for his lighter and pack of cigarettes. He pulled one out and lit it.

"Got one for me?" Alana asked.

"Of course."

Bacon handed her a Parliament. They sat on the dock, huddled together smoking. Alana rested her head on Brandon's shoulder. For a moment they simply existed.

"Do you think we're going to die out here?" she asked.

"I don't know, I just want the sun to come up."

"Me too."

"It's only one-thirty. We've got four more hours till dawn," he replied, taking a puff of his cig.

"Let's go back to camp after we finish these and make a fire," Alana whispered.

"I like that idea."

They gathered kindling and began to build a fire with the logs they brought from the mainland. The fire grew in size and the flames danced off the tent walls beside it. The two friends sat in silence, with the weight of their situation.

"I just wanna go home," Alana stated flatly.

***

The night passed and eventually, dawn approached. The birds began to sing and traces of sunlight crept between the cracks in the evergreens. Alana and Bacon watched the sunrise, grateful they were alive to see its beauty.

"That's the most gorgeous sunrise I've ever seen," Alana noted.

"Yes, it is," Bacon replied in agreement. Before they knew it, it was full morning and they were cooking breakfast. They talked and hatched a plan to find Spencer and Chelsea.

"Maybe they fell down a ravine or something and we can't hear them yelling?" Bacon suggested.

"It's certainly possible. I just don't understand why they would've ventured that far up in elevation, it's not like there's a pathway."

"I think there is a trail that leads to the very top of that overlook over there," Bacon said as he pointed at the highest outcropping, a jagged cliff that protruded out from a massive slab of granite.

"Do you know how to get there?"

"Nope. I've only been here once, we came on a retreat at camp before Derek and I got kicked out." Bacon choked up, thinking about his friend who was now dead. Tears slowly trickled down his face.

Bacon wiped his gaunt cheeks and continued speaking. "I remember kids saying back in the day there was a trail around the other side of the island by the inlet and small waterfall."

"Well, the sun is up, let's go. If anything, we can scan the area for anything unusual and also get an idea of what the island looks like. We can hide out up there, too, if needed. In case whoever that was comes back for us," Alana advised.

"If they do, we'll be ready."

"We need to be. We can ambush them if we have to," she said as she pointed the gun at the beach and squinted her eye with confidence.

"Follow me. I can find the trail. I heard it's even marked in some places," Bacon said.

Alana ran behind him and they began their search for the forgotten path. "Follow the leader!" she shouted.

"It's on!" he replied eagerly. Despite the situation, they were trying to make the best of it. The duo knew it was their only chance of survival, they weren't out of the woods yet.

Together they sauntered on the sand in hopes of finding not only the trail but maybe their friends, as well. They hiked in silence for a bit. They each smoked a cigarette, keeping a short distance between each other once they entered the forest. It didn't take long before they ventured off into the shade and away from the beach. As they tiptoed through the underbrush, they stumbled upon the gruesome scene. Bacon almost tripped over Chelsea's leg, which was sticking out from a bunch of lush ferns.

"It's Chelsea and Spencer!" Bacon screamed in horror.

He instantly began throwing up all over the forest floor. The chunks of puke gathered on the intricate earth patterns etched below.

"Oh my God, don't look!" he shouted as he grabbed Alana to pull her away from the horrific images before them. Chelsea and Spencer were both naked with fishing hooks gouged into their skin. Various lures were on their face, ears, stomachs, necks, and chests. They were strung together with fishing line and the string ran through each hook, protruding from their flesh.

"Who would do such a terrible thing?" Alana cried out, then covered her face and fell to the earth. She crawled as fast as she could away from the dead bodies. She managed to pull herself to her feet and took off.

"We need to get off this island, now!" Bacon insisted. He fumbled around his pockets for his lighter and papers.

"What are you doing?" Alana asked.

"I need to smoke a joint before I lose my mind."

"Are you crazy, how can you think about getting stoned right now?"

"Hey don't judge me, I'm surviving."

"Whatever," Alana muttered softly. Her patience with Brandon vanished. She was feeling alone and isolated. Fear was winning and hope was dwindling.

With each second that ticked by, Alana grew closer to the harsh reality she may die on Mirror Island.

# CHAPTER EIGHT

"We need to go back past them. I'm so sorry, Alana, but we have to if we want to get to the trail. I'll guide you by it, just close your eyes. Don't look at them. Cover your face when we go by."

Bacon directed her past the terrifying display further into the dense wilderness. Trudging along full of trepidation, they were greeted by a vibrant green meadow. It was delicate and fertile. Grass grew from the forest floor with ferns and flora sprouting from below.

Then they heard it. A strange sound.

"Is that a fucking rooster?" Alana asked in confusion.

"That is a rooster."

At that moment, they were met by a flock of dozens of bantam chickens. Several roosters and hens were scouring the meadow, mechanically pecking at the ground. Some hens were black with gray specks, while others were white like puffy snowballs with black tail feathers. There were yellow hens mixed in and the roosters were white or multicolored with gorgeous plumes. The birds crowed and hollered in the morning dew. Bacon ran at them in hopes of catching one, but they vanished in a flash, flying up to the branches.

"I had no idea chicken could fly that high," Bacon muttered in awe.

Alana gazed at the trees. "Bantams can fly very high and far when they want. We have them on our farm. There are probably eggs around here. We should search for a nest, look around the base of the firs."

"We could use the eggs after the camp got ransacked and our food spoiled. Besides, we're fucking trapped with no way out right now," Bacon said while observing the flock in the trees.

"No shit, Sherlock. Help me find a nest."

Together they searched the undergrowth for eggs to eat. Minutes ticked by and they weren't finding a thing. An image off in the distance caught Bacon's eye. He noticed a gently used path and followed it before he stumbled upon another altar of baby doll heads and animal skeletons. These totems, however, were more intricate and incorporated more plastic body parts. Several types of severed animal bones were glued to each toy head. Intestines and blood covered the ground. It was obvious someone, or something, had recently devoured or gutted an animal right where they were standing.

Maggots and flies crawled and fluttered around the animal entrails. Bacon went to run back to Alana but noticed the sliver of a makeshift shelter in the distance. He wandered over to the tiny outbuilding. It had three walls and a roof with a mattress under it. Next to the bed was an end table with a bowl of eggs tucked inside of it. He ran over and grabbed the container, darting back to Alana with his discovery. When he returned, she was delighted with his find but mortified to hear he also saw more creepy totems and signs of what appeared like an animal slaughter.

"Whose eggs are these, you think?" Bacon asked.

Alana stared at him dead in the face. "Probably the person who killed our friends and took off with the boat."

"You think so?" he inquired with fear.

"Who else?" she said, pinching her forehead in frustration.

Bacon wrinkled his nose and created a ripple across his young, tan face. "Lewis Ford."

Alana laughed. "Lewis Ford is merely a story we told when we were kids. We all know he either died out here, alone and desperate, or he ran away and started a new life far from his abusive father. The harsh reality is, he's probably dead," she stated without fanfare.

"Regardless of whose shelter it is, we have eggs now. I'll carry the bowl and will tread lightly," Bacon said as he put his pack on.

"This way!" he declared as he pointed toward a stretch of fir trees that etched their way around a giant boulder.

"After you." Alana gestured with her hand.

Step by step, they traversed the gradual incline. Clouds rolled in and covered up the sun, creating blankets of shade on the craggy outcroppings. A light mist appeared as fog seeped through the canopies. The temperature dropped and they put their hoods up as rain began to fall. They delicately ascended the rough terrain, being careful not to slip as the trail narrowed.

"This is the way to the overhang. See the gold spray paint?" Bacon asked while running his hand over the rockface.

Alana paused and examined the air. "Thank God."

"We're getting close," Bacon told her. His eyes were shifting side to side with each step he took.

The rain poured down as they reached the top and went to the overlook. The fog was thick and they couldn't see anything. It was a murky cloak, a vast tarp of grey that obstructed their view of Mirror Island.

"Damn it!" Alana yelled in defeat.

"This is why they call it Mirror Island. Because the fog gets so thick, you can't even see your reflection in a mirror," Bacon explained, peering out at the endless quilt of grey clouds and heavy fog.

"Check out this path," Alana said as she scampered down a well-worn trail to a covered spot.

"Nice," Bacon whispered under his breath.

"We're hanging out here until this fog clears out," Alana told him with a sense of urgency.

"I like it," he agreed.

The two sat under the arched boulder until the rain ceased. In a matter of time, the fog dissipated and the sun was out. Rays of light projected across the Washington landscapes.

"It's noon. I'm surprised we haven't seen any hikers or campers of any kind. How are we the only ones out here when it's spring break?" Bacon questioned, glancing at his Fossil watch.

"Maybe folks around here know better," Alana suggested.

"Maybe you're right."

They sat perched on the cliff observing the beach below.

"We need to sleep while we're safe. We can hear if anyone comes by boat or foot. Let's take advantage of it while we can," Alana said to Bacon. Her brown eyes were heavily fixed on her chaotic surroundings.

"Should we both sleep?" Bacon asked, lighting a cigarette.

Alana pulled her sleeping bag off her daypack. "I think it's fine, we need sleep so we can think straight."

Bacon followed suit and unraveled his royal blue bag. "Works for me."

A few hours drifted by and Alana awoke to find herself alone and Bacon was not in his sleeping bag. "Fuckin Bacon," she muttered to herself as she got up from the ground and scanned around.

She was startled by him as he bolted around the corner of the rock face by the trail. His eyes were big and his expression was wide and curious. A crooked smile emerged from the farthest corners of his thin-rimmed mouth.

"You look like you've seen a ghost, what happened?" she questioned, wondering why he was acting so strange.

"Me?" he replied as he pointed at himself.

"No, the guy behind you," she answered sarcastically.

"There's someone behind me?" he said as he began laughing. He turned around swiftly, stumbling with each swivel.

"Are you high?" she asked him, grimacing.

"Kinda?"

"Well, you looked stoned as hell," Alana told him, her voice tight.

"I did smoke some weed, but I took two tabs of x."

"Are you shitting me?" she shouted.

"Yeah, I feel fucking great. Figured it would make me feel better. That's why I came here, anyway. To roll through these rugged hills like a jagged little pill. You get it," he joked.

"Great, now on top of everything, I'm babysitting a moron. You're such a child, Brandon."

"Hey, speak for yourself, pretty lady, I'm not the one marinating in pity. If I'm going out here, I'm going out on cloud nine."

"You can't keep your head straight for one hour, can you? What the hell is wrong with you?"

"A lot of things. Right now I feel like a jellyfish riding a lawnmower through the desert. Squishy and mechanical, like an engine. You should take one, or two, like me."

"I'm good. I'd like to survive Mirror Island, not get consumed by it," Alana grumbled as she stormed ahead of Bacon.

"The stars look like monkeys flying through the sky, like in the Barrel of Monkeys game. Do you ever play that shit? I miss that game."

# CHAPTER NINE

"**B**arrel of monkeys? Jesus, Bacon. I can't believe you'd take that shit right now. I need you level-headed, not high in the stars playing a Barrel of Monkeys like a toddler."

"I think that games for ages three and up," he replied with a chuckle.

"Seriously? What's wrong with you? Why you gotta pull this shit?"

"Because we're living in hell and I needed a release. If we're going to die out here at least I'm going out having some fun," he answered as he lifted his hands to the air and twirled like an uncoordinated ballerina.

"I'm exhausted and now I need to keep my eye on you. I was hoping to get more sleep while the sun was still up. We'll have to be on guard all night."

"Go back to sleep, I'm fine," Bacon said with a twinkle in his eye.

He was beginning to rub his hands all over his chest and stomach in slow circular motion. He waved his body back and forth.

"Are you sure? You look like you are rolling pretty hard," Alana insisted. She glared at Brandon. His eyes were giant and black.

"Your aura is so beautiful, Alana, it's like a greenish-blue color. Oh, I just realized green and blue together is *glue*."

"You're dumb as fucking nails. I'm going back to sleep for thirty minutes. Please don't do anything stupid and do *not* take any more ecstasy, damn it," Alana demanded.

"Yes, mother."

She rolled her eyes, yanked the sleeping bag over her head, and went back to sleep. Time ticked by and Alana slept longer than she intended. When she awoke, she was happy to find Bacon lying on top of his sleeping bag and shifting around like a squirming fish out of water.

"Are you ok?" she asked with a look of scrutiny.

"I feel like an octopus," he replied, wiggling his arms spastically to resemble tentacles.

"What time is it?"

Bacon looked at his watch for a moment or two, his eyes bugged out of his face as he read the time. "It's four o'clock. Twenty minutes till four-twenty!" he exclaimed.

"You don't need anything else in your system right now, damn it, Bacon! You're a child," she yelled in his face. Her frustration was building and she was growing concerned that they may die out in the wilderness.

"Are you mad at me?" he asked with a faint whisper.

"Yes, but I can't blame you," she admitted.

"You want one?"

Alana shook her head in irritation. "No, one of us has to stay alert. We need to pack up and head down the trail back to the campsite. Are you alright to hike back?"

Bacon was focused on the environment around him. "Yeah, I'm cool."

"Follow me, I'm leading the way now," Alana ordered as she began her trek down the path.

Dusk was rapidly approaching, they needed to finish the hike and get to camp well before sunset. Bacon was becoming a hazard for Alana. Her annoyance with him and his choices only continued to grow as they hiked. They reached the beach before dusk, then quickly gathered firewood and prepared the food they had left. Alana was unfortunately stuck doing the majority of the work as Bacon located his CD player and was jamming tunes in his headphones, dancing around the beach like a character.

She knew he'd be crashing soon and his comedown was going to be brutal. Once his serotonin levels plummeted and reality set back in, he was going to be in for it. The collapse would be heavy and severe. Alana was dreading it and she knew she'd be dealing with his depression when she might need him the most.

"We're getting low on food, we need to start thinking of how we're going to get off this island tomorrow if no one shows up in the morning. Bacon, can you hear me? Take the headphones off!" she yelled as she motioned at him. He was deep into the psychedelic music that played in his bulky headphones.

"Bacon!" she screamed in his face.

"What? Sorry. What's up?"

"We're low on food, we have to get out of here tomorrow," she insisted.

"God will carry us out of here," he whispered to himself.

Alana was furious. She clenched her fists and for a moment she thought about hitting him in the face. After all, he deserved it. "God will carry us out of here? This is insane, you are so high. You do realize you're going to crash hard and you're going to feel like shit tonight. I hope you do and when it happens, don't come crying to me."

Bacon didn't respond, he just put his headphones back on and ignored her.

Alana thought about abandoning him and setting out on her own, but she knew she needed to keep an eye on him and wondered if it would all be the same in the end, regardless. She'd already lost three of her friends and she didn't want to lose another. Her heart ached and she was losing her grip on reality.

"Shit, my batteries are dead, you got any double As, Alana?" Bacon asked.

"No. The sun is about to fully set. Can you at least help me gather some kindling and wood to dry around the fire, so we have enough for tonight?"

"Yeah, I can do that," he replied reluctantly.

Alana drifted toward the woods in search of kindling and logs to dry out. When she returned to the beach, she noticed Bacon over by his bag.

"What are you doing?" she asked him with fury.

He ignored her again, quickly pulling a plastic bag out and shoved a small tablet in his mouth.

"What the fuck did you just take? Did you just take more x? Are you kidding me?"

Alana was furious. She shoved Bacon onto the ground.

"What the fuck?" he yelled from the sand.

"You're on your own, I'm done," she said as she ran to the dock with her pack and the gun.

"Cool with me. I don't need you, anyway. Dumb bitch," he muttered as he pulled out a cigarette and searched his pockets for his orange lighter. It took a moment, but he eventually located it in his flannel pocket. He lit his cigarette and blew on the ember.

Alana sat on the tattered dock and tried to fight back the oppressive sorrow washing over her like the waves that rippled against the weathered structure. Shadows from the trees crept along the wood planks. A huge part of her felt guilty. She knew Bacon was struggling just like her. She pushed her pride aside and went back over to the campsite.

"Hey," she said. The flames of the fire flickered on her face as she held her head low.

"Hey."

"Here's some water, you're gonna need it," she offered as she handed him a purple Nalgene bottle.

"Thanks. I'm sorry you gotta babysit me. I... I just..." Bacon began to cry. The overwhelming sadness of the loss of his friends and their dire situation began to overtake him.

"It's ok. Really. Bacon, we've known each other since kindergarten. You're more of a brother to me than my actual brother is. I fucking love you, man. This is scary shit."

"I love you too, Alana," he said as he wiped the tears from his dirty face.

The sounds of a boat off in the distance startled them.

"That sounds like Spencer's boat," Alana said.

"It does," he replied abruptly.

"Grab your shit and let's go, we gotta get into the woods fast. Let's try and find that makeshift shelter by the meadow. We have to creep. I need your help right now, Bacon."

Together they vanished into the darkness of the surrounding forest. They trudged through the thicket and struggled to locate the faint trial that led to the meadow. The boat engine was getting louder and louder.

"Hurry, Bacon, we gotta find a place to hide and be silent," she whispered.

Bacon was lagging, slowing their pace as he fluttered like leaves caught in the wind. "I'm coming," he mumbled while he struggled to keep a consistent stride.

The darkness grew as they navigated their way further and further into the dense wilderness.

"I don't hear the boat anymore, they must be on shore," Alana voiced.

"I think if we go this way, we can get to the shelter," Bacon replied while motioning toward an opening in the evergreens.

"I'll follow you, don't let me regret this!"

Bacon led the way as the duo progressed through the scattered greenwood. "I see a deer path or some shit," he murmured.

"Let's take it," Alana responded.

"Cool."

The path went on for much longer than they expected. Minutes passed by, before they knew it they'd been walking on a trail for close to ten minutes.

"Thank God for moonlight," Alana said to herself.

Bacon began to chuckle.

"Something funny?" she asked impatiently.

"Sorry, starting to feel it again," Bacon said with a soft giggle.

"Just be quiet and stay on the path, it has to end soon."

"You wanna lead the way now?" Bacon asked.

"No, I wanna keep my eye on you."

"I can't believe this trail is still going. I can't imagine where this will lead us," he told Alana, reducing his pace to a steady stride before coming to a complete halt.

"What are you doing? Don't stop. We gotta keep going, this trail is giving us distance from whoever is after us."

"I'm tired, though," Bacon whimpered.

"Tough shit, keep on rolling!"

"Pun intended?" he asked with a smirk.

Alana laughed out loud. "Clever, I'll admit, you dumbass."

"Shit, more creepy dolls," Bacon mumbled, placing his eyes on the most intricate totems they'd seen. The stake was a whole tree and it had bigger doll heads. They were almost human size.

"Those loom like American Girl Doll heads," Alana uttered in terror.

Animal bones were scattered about at the base of the totem. It must've stood eight feet high and had over twelve human-sized doll heads and plastic body parts nestled between a plethora of muted deer skulls.

"How are there so many deer skulls? There aren't even deer on the island. There must be twelve on that totem alone," Alana pointed out as she panned her eyes down the altar. That's when something caught her eye at the base of the structure.

"That looks like a human skeleton and skull," Bacon stuttered.

"That's a really old skeleton, those bones are incredibly aged. They have lichen and moss growing on them," she replied in shock as she examined the lush green forest flora that was covering the human remains in several places.

Both Alana and Bacon stood amongst the corpse in silence. Their flashlights waved along the shrine of death and human decay.

"Who do you think it is? Lewis Ford? Did we just discover his body? I knew it!" Bacon exclaimed.

"It's possible, but if that's him, we need to get out of here! I can't take this much death anymore... What are you doing? Don't touch it, Bacon!"

The skeleton was sitting as if it died peacefully meditating beneath the altar. The skull and ribcage were still showing beneath the contrast of green hues of scattered forest debris. Bacon continued to poke and prod the skull with his hand until it detached and fell onto the forest floor. He picked it up off of the ground and stared at it intensely. Alana could tell he was beginning to feel the drug pumping through his veins. He held the skull in his palm and began to laugh.

"What if I skullfucked it right now, what would you do? Would that gross you out?"

"Skullfucked it? Seriously, what are you, like twelve? I'm out of here, you're deranged," Alana responded in disgust. She couldn't help but recognize a part of her was slightly amused, however. As time eroded, humor seemed to be the only thing they had left to hold on to. Suddenly, something fluttered in the trees above them.

"Did you hear that?" Alana whispered.

"Yeah, sounds like something in the canopy over there, above us." Bacon pointed to a fir tree to their left and looked up. Alana shined her flashlight up into the branches and screamed like a banshee when she saw the man's hairy face. He was unkempt, feral-looking. His skin was weathered and rough, his clothing outdated and tattered. He stood still in the trees for several moments before he jumped to the ground.

"Run!" Alana exclaimed.

In an instant, they both took off back down the trail.

"I'm behind you!" Bacon screamed. He let out a heavy sigh as he followed behind Alana closely. With each step, they both were breathing harder and harder. Time slowed down and the forest seemed to go quiet.

# CHAPTER TEN

"**D**id you see that?" Alana asked Bacon once they slowed their pace to a halt.

"I saw a man with a big beard sitting up in the trees, watching us," he replied, trying to catch his breath.

"That's exactly what I saw," she answered in shock.

"I don't think he followed us," Bacon mumbled.

Alana was trembling so much, her voice shook. "He looked almost primitive, feral even."

"Like a caveman. Oh man, I'm way too high for this," Bacon interjected as he paced back and forth.

"Whose fault is that?" Alana replied flatly.

They stood there bickering for a bit before Bacon wandered off. Alana turned around to go further down the trail but after a moment or two, she turned around to find herself alone. Bacon was nowhere to be seen.

"Bacon, Bacon, where the hell are you? Damn it, Brandon," she whispered.

He wasn't around. In only a few seconds, Bacon had managed to drift off the trail on his own accord.

Alana searched tirelessly for him in the area they were in but didn't see him and was becoming increasingly more worried about his safety, as well as her own. Panic swelled inside of her as she began to feel uneasy. She couldn't help but feel like eyes were watching her. She hoped maybe Bacon was messing with her, however, she assumed it was wishful thinking.

Alone and isolated, Alana wandered the scenic landscape quietly under the moonlight. She stumbled upon another small makeshift shelter. This one, though, was simple and had no signs of obscurity. She hunkered down for a while and snacked on an energy bar she'd stashed in her bag.

*How am I going to get myself out of here?* she thought to herself. She was beginning to fall apart. Teardrops filled her eyes as she searched for the sketchbook in her pack and pulled it out along with a pen. She cut her headlamp on and began to write a letter to her family.

*Dear Mom, Dad, David, and Amber,*

*I love you all so much. I'm so sorry and cannot even begin to explain how overcome with regret I am. I don't know who is after us and what we did to deserve this, but as I write this, Spencer, Chelsea, and Derek are dead. They were all brutally murdered on Mirror Island. Brandon and I have been hiding in the forest for two days but he wandered off, and I have no idea where he is. I just want to come home. I wish I was back at the house, watching movies with David and*

*Amber. This was such a bad idea and we should have followed Jenna's lead. She pleaded with us not to come, to turn around and go home like she did. Instead, we mocked her. In turn, it has cost us our lives. Life is fragile and time is finite. Please know, I did everything I could in my life to make you all proud of me. My heart breaks when I think about what you're about to go through. I never meant for any of this to happen. Please, trust me about this. I love you all with every bit of my heart.*

*Love, hugs, and endless kisses,*

*Alana*

She closed her sketchpad, placed it back in her bag, and began to weep. She sat there for a bit marinating in her guilt. "Please, God, help me," she whispered to herself. The wind rustled in the trees.

Out of nowhere, she felt a hand grab her. In an instant, she was flung to the ground. Alana went to scream but she was paralyzed with fear. Waves of horror undulated through her entire body. She kicked and tried to run, but the man had her pinned and was choking her. She started to gag and struggled to breathe, feeling her throat closing. She heard screams all around her, howling cries that pierced her ears. The yells increased in volume and size. At that moment, everything faded to black and she was floating above her body.

She gazed down at herself laying lifeless on the forest floor. A man in a hood was standing over her. She was dying. Higher and higher her body rose until she was a part of the clouds. She felt herself evaporate and become a part of the aether above.

*At least death came quickly,* she thought to herself as she dissolved into emptiness. The fear eroded and she was now nothing, merely a ripple in space.

All of a sudden, Alana gasped and shrieked, sitting up. "Huh," she muttered, confused by what was happening.

She jumped to her feet and gathered her senses. "It was only a dream," she said to herself. She looked at her surroundings and thought, *I must have dozed off after writing the letter.*

She'd slept for a couple of hours. It was now well after midnight and she was unsure what she should do next. Discombobulated and scared, she continued to hide out in the small shelter until something jumped onto the roof of the outbuilding, startling her. She took off as fast as she could with her pack on, dodging trees left and right. Her ankle snapped as she shuffled by a patch of rocks.

"Ouch!" she yelled while grasping her ankle.

*No, please, don't be broken,* she thought.

Alana tried to stand up but fell back over. She hurried to her feet and began hobbling as fast as her ankle would let her out of the forest. It hurt like hell, but she pushed the pain aside and let the adrenaline take over.

"I am *not* going to die out here," she said out loud.

Scrambling with everything she had, Alana fought to move as quickly as she could. The fir trees were beginning to thin and she was approaching flatter terrain. She felt her ankle give out again and she toppled down.

She looked up to see a middle-aged man with a beard peering over her. His face was dirty and his eyes baggy. He appeared as if he hadn't slept in years. He had a deep scar on the left side of his face, running from his ear to his mouth. He threw all of his body weight on top of Alana. She struggled to get him off her, but he was easily twice her size.

The man shoved his hairy fingers around Alana's throat and pressed as hard as he could. With all his strength, he held her down firmly. Her legs kicked and flailed around. The man paused and reached into his pocket, pulling out a fishing knife. He went to stab her in the stomach. At that moment, Alana managed to kick the knife out of his hand and into the darkness. He slammed her hard onto the cold earth below. She let out a groan as her body made a loud thud. Again, he pressed with everything he had until she started to fade out. She was drifting in and out of consciousness.

For a brief second her true self rose to the surface. *My dream was an omen.*

That's when she heard the gunshots echo through the air. One, two, three in a row. The noise was deafening, echoing through the island. The man collapsed on top of Alana and blood saturated her clothing. She wiggled her way from under the man's lifeless body to see another man in a hood, holding a rifle to his shoulder.

"Are you ok?" he asked her calmly.

Alana then recognized him as the man she and Bacon saw hiding in the trees, watching them from above. She scooted away from him and the other man.

"Please, don't hurt me," she said, her voice trembling with fear.

"I'm not going to hurt you. I'm here to help. That man was going to kill you like he killed your friends. I didn't mean to scare you. My name is Lewis. Lewis Ford."

"Lewis Ford? Oh, I figured you were long since dead," Alana answered.

"Everyone does. I like it that way, honestly. Come with me, we need to get you cleaned up and that ankle addressed. I have a first aid kit at my home. You're safe there. Trust me," he said to her in a sincere and comforting tone.

# CHAPTER ELEVEN

**B**ack on Orcas Island, the local police had been receiving several calls for days about a strange and suspicious man in a worn, green raincoat. He was described as being in his late forties or early fifties with a dark, scraggly beard.

The most recent was from a man at the Jordison Wharf on Orcas Island, who reported seeing a creepy guy in a raincoat dumping a body into the ocean from a bay boat. The police quickly were on the scene at the wharf and a deep dive search was underway.

Search and rescue teams were beginning to scour the water surrounding the several islands on the coast of Washington state. Chelsea's parents called local police when they didn't hear from their daughter for over forty-eight hours. Once her mother realized no one could get in touch with the children and none of the other parents had heard from their kids for days, she became very worried.

Another report the police received was two days prior, when a gentleman said his old pontoon boat was stolen from his dock and he saw a bearded man in a raincoat taking off into the moonlight with it.

That call coincided with others from residents on Orcas Island a night prior of a man with a beard in a green raincoat standing in the middle of the street, screaming and crying. Various residents called and stated they were driving by a guy running manically down the street in distress, while others reported seeing a man crying on the side of the road, holding something. Some folks said he was embracing a person while others called in insisting they saw a man walking down the road, carrying a dead animal.

Back on Mirror Island, Alana was settling in at Lewis's home. He'd built a well-constructed and hidden cabin deep in the thickest part of the forest. It was quaint and cozy once she got past all the severed baby doll heads and animal bones decorating the circumference of the residence. The closer to his home they got, the more threatening the totems appeared. The ones closest to his house were covered in pentagrams and were engraved with evil messages. There were decaying animal guts and bones at the base of the altars.

"What's with all the baby doll heads, animal bones, and flesh everywhere? Are you a Satanist? I saw lots of pentagrams and triple sixes," Alana asked with hesitation.

"Well, for starters, the pentagram isn't exactly satanic, but to answer your question, no. I don't worship Satan, however, I live alone in the wilderness and have for a long time. You're the first person I've spoken to in twenty years. I need to do something to scare people off. Most of the doll parts I get from the dump. I take a rowboat to the other islands and mainlands monthly. I've been doing so the entire time I've lived out here," he told her.

"Makes sense," she replied as they entered the cabin. Inside, it was simple, yet warm and cozy. She was immediately greeted by a yellow lab, who ran over in pure excitement.

"That's Tacoma. She's sweet as can be. A very good girl," Lewis said as he petted her on her long face.

"She's so pretty," Alana murmured as she rubbed Tacoma's head and snuggled her. She was so relieved to be warm, safe, and cuddled up with a big, sweet dog.

"It's a shame someone dumped her here and left her to die alone. It's incredibly cruel, only a demon would do such a thing. Sadly, she's not the first. I had a dog for thirteen years, who was also dumped here.

"River was his name. He was a border collie and an incredible mountain dog. I loved him very much and was with him till the end. I also have a cat around here somewhere. Luna, where are you, girl?" he said, searching the dimly lit cabin.

Alana heard the sound of a tiny bell and a beautiful calico cat came walking up, proud as could be. She went over to Alana and rubbed against her, purring incessantly. "Aw, pretty kitty. She was dumped too?" Alana asked.

"Yes, she was a young kitten, too. So cruel."

"It certainly is, how fortunate they are to have you here to take care of them," she replied.

"Humans are shit sometimes," Lewis said.

"Isn't that the truth?" Alana agreed as Luna climbed into her lap.

Lewis went over to a cabinet in the farthest left corner of the cabin. There was a small fireplace, as well as a big pot with a fire under it to boil food.

"Here, let me see that ankle." Lewis took some time to examine her fracture, other bruises, and injuries.

"You seem to know what you're doing," Alana said, her eyes closely watching his every move.

"I've been living alone in the wilderness for twenty years. I have to know what I'm doing," he replied.

"Why did you come out here to live in a harsh existence fighting against extreme elements?" Alana inquired.

"I was young when I ran away. Seventeen. My mother died and I was alone with my abusive father with no siblings. He beat the shit out of my mother and me. I had to get away or I was going to kill him. I didn't want to become another prison number. So, I fled here. I stole a dinghy from a nearby wharf and came here in the spring of 1978. Originally, I didn't plan on staying long but over time it just became my life. I got used to it. I learned to love and appreciate how simple life in nature is. My relationship with the wilderness grows stronger every day I live out here. At this point, it's all I know. Up until you and your friends showed up, it was quiet and peaceful."

"Sorry about that. What about the skeleton me and my..." At that moment Alana remembered she needed to find Bacon. She continued, "My friend and I found a skeleton covered in moss and lichen at the base of one of your altars."

"Oh, yeah, that. I have no idea who that is. That body was here when I got here. At least, I think it was. I'd been here for a few years before I discovered it. I felt sad for whoever it was, so I put them in a peaceful position at the base of that evergreen tree. This was well before the baby doll totems. I wasn't having close encounters with camp kids back then. That all started in the late eighties," he answered.

"My friend Brandon. He's still out there. We need to find him. We got separated when he wandered off."

"We can look for him, but we'll have to wait until the morning. In the meantime, you need to rest. I can tell you haven't been sleeping. You're safe here, please. Rest," he insisted as he motioned toward a bed.

"I'm so tired," Alana mentioned, observing the dimly lit space. The room was quaint and cozy despite its minimal decor.

"Please, sleep. Luna may curl up with you or even sleep on you. We'll look for your friend once the sun rises."

"Ok. Lewis, I really can't thank you enough for saving my life."

"It's the least I can do. Get some rest."

Dawn came and Lewis and Alana headed out to look for Bacon. They started their search in the dense forests and Lewis led her around various ravines, hills, secret trails, and deer paths.

"I know every inch of this island like the back of my hand," he said as they hiked through a field of ferns. He continued speaking as he held his ear to the air. "Listen, I can hear Garcia crowing!" he proclaimed.

"Garcia?"

"That's one of my roosters who sticks to this area."

"*Your* roosters?" she inquired.

"Yup. I take care of all the chickens here. They help me eat, so I feed them. The bantams were here when I arrived and over the years I've watched countless generations of chickens strut all over this island. I catch and trap the hens the best I can. All the chickens are subject to being picked off by eagles, hawks, owls, and osprey, so to preserve the hens, I try to catch a few to the cage."

"So, that was your bowl of eggs we stole. I'm so sorry," she replied.

"Certainly it was, but it's ok. I have plenty of eggs, that is only one of the many makeshift stations I have littered around the island."

They trudged on in search of Bacon, but there was no sign of him anywhere. It was as if he vanished like a ghost. Lewis knew every tree and crevice of the island. The hours trickled by and Bacon was nowhere to be found. Alana grew anxious.

"We're never going to find him," she said.

"We will, trust me. I know this island, this is my life. We'll find your friend. I just hope he's alive."

Lewis led Alana around several groves of fir trees, lush meadows of ferns, and tall grasses, but everywhere they searched led nowhere. There wasn't a sign of Brandon anywhere. No headphones, backpack, shirt, or shoes. He'd completely vanished into thin air.

Another couple of hours cruised by and they emerged out of the woods onto the beach. They were near the dock. Alana recognized their campsite and saw Spencer's family boat moored at the dock. It looked deserted and desolate. She ran over onto the boat to find an old dead woman hunched over in the captain's chair. Her skin was covered in maggots and her flesh was rotting off her bones. Flies were everywhere, the buzzing incredibly loud. Alana went to escape from the sight but puked over the side into the ocean, instead.

Lewis ran aboard and discovered the corpse. "Let's get you out of here," he said as he moved her away from the boat and down the dock to the beach.

"Who is that woman? This is my friend's boat," Alana muttered in confusion.

"We need to get you away from this, come with me," Lewis said while leading Alana away from the old corpse.

"It looks like she's been dead for days, what on Earth?" Alana cried out in fear.

"Don't look," Lewis voiced.

She was shaking violently. "I don't understand what's going on," she confessed to Lewis.

"I'm not sure, dear, but let's get you somewhere safe."

# CHAPTER TWELVE

**B**ack on the mainland, the local police were still searching for the missing high school seniors. The teens kept their journey to Mirror Island a secret from their families, so the search had not spread that far out yet.

They were combing through the wilderness surrounding Orcas Island and the coast of Washington State without a clue until the police chief got a call from a young woman in Tacoma named Jenna.

The Orcas Island police quickly sent out a team to Mirror Island and also notified the Coast Guard, who dispatched a unit to the island.

Alana and Lewis were trying to make sense of the recently deceased woman on the bay boat. She was old, well into her eighties. Her hair was thin and gray. She was incredibly small and frail.

"You're sure you don't know who that old woman is?" he asked.

"I have no idea who she is. I've never seen her in my life," Alana replied, trying to look at the woman, but the sight of decay made it hard for her to look for long.

"I don't understand who this man is and why he attacked my friends and me," she stated with confusion.

"And why would he be carrying a dead woman on board?" Lewis questioned.

"He probably killed her, too," Alana suggested.

Just then, they heard the sounds of police boats and rescue helicopters approaching.

"That sounds like help. I can't stay with you, Alana. I'm sorry."

"I understand. I can't thank you enough for saving my life, Lewis. You have a beautiful soul," she said as she hugged him. He hadn't felt human contact and affection in over twenty years. His heart sang.

"It's my pleasure, Alana." He paused for a moment and then spoke again, his voice soft and pleading, "Can you please be sure not to tell anyone about me? I've lived here in solitude for years and I'd like to keep it that way."

"Of course, Lewis. Your secret is safe with me."

"Thank you, Alana. Now go!" he muttered as he motioned her toward the beach and took off into the dense forest wilderness.

When the police and coast guard reached the island, they rushed to Alana and began to scour the area. The police chief was horrified by the scene when he saw the dead old woman on the boat. It didn't take long for the cops to find Spencer and Chelsea's massacred bodies. Alana was surrounded by officers and chartered off Mirror Island to safety.

Waves of joy and sorrow overtook her. She was secure and finally going home, however, she'd lost all of her friends. The moment was bittersweet. She reflected on her time on Mirror Island as she watched seagulls flying in the sunset. When the rescue boat reached the shore, she was taken to the Orcas Island police station where she was immediately interrogated.

Police Chief Warren Watkins took his hat off and placed it on the table. He reached for his cup of stale coffee and took a sip. He made a face of disgust at the cup before he spoke.

"Alana, sweetheart, I'm glad you're safe. We found Spencer and Chelsea's bodies, as well as the man who was shot to death in the forest. We also found the Barrett family bay boat with the deceased elderly woman aboard. We're still looking for Brandon and Derek's bodies. I know you've been through a lot over the last few days. But I need you to tell me what happened. Start from the beginning, please," the chief requested.

"Sure. Well.." Alana's eyes swelled up and filled with tears as she continued to speak. "The plan from the beginning was to go to Mirror Island and camp for a couple of days. We left Tacoma early Saturday evening and arrived on Orcas Island later that night."

"What time did you get on the island?" he asked.

"Maybe nine or nine-thirty?" she replied nervously.

"Ok, thank you. You may continue."

"We hit a dog or something before we got to Spencer's cabin. A few miles from his family's house. We pulled over shortly after because we had a flat. Then we got to Spencer's maybe at ten that night, it was already dark and the fog was heavy."

"Wait, you hit a dog or some kind of animal? You're not sure what it was?" Warren asked with strong intent as his mind began to race.

"Yeah, we didn't stop right away. Spencer didn't want to. But less than maybe a mile down the road we got a flat, so we did pull over."

The chief took a slow sip of his cold coffee. "Did you see the animal?"

"Kinda. I saw some fur and the others agreed they did, too, but like I said, it was dark and foggy. It was hard to tell what it was," Alana replied with her head down.

"Do you know what road you were on or if there were any landmarks nearby?"

"I don't know road names around here, but I know we had just passed a creepy old house with a dilapidated roof and a little pond in front of it. There's a sign that says, 'duck eggs'. I remember because Bacon laughed when we drove by it and said, 'Duck eggs, fuck eggs.'"

Warren's eyes lit up. That's *Lucious Way*. I'll be right back," he mumbled as he walked out of his office rapidly. He was gone for several minutes, then he came back appearing flushed.

"Spencer was driving?" he asked Alana.

"Yes, he was driving. Chelsea was in the passenger seat. Bacon and Derek were in the captain's seats. I sat by myself in the back of the Quest."

The chief looked down at a clipboard with notes and photographs. His hands trembled as he rubbed his freckled face and then his thick red mustache. "Alana..." he paused, took a hefty deep breath, then continued to speak with caution, "Spencer didn't hit an animal."

"What do you mean, what did he hit, then?" she inquired, her brain trying to remember what she saw that night.

"A person."

"A person? It couldn't have been. I saw fur, we all did," she countered as she began to shake, her eyes widened and shock set in.

"The old woman that was dead on Spencer's family boat, that's who you guys ran over. Her name is Margaret Murphy. She was 81. She lived in the home with the duck eggs for sale with her son Christopher. She has dementia. She was walking *Lucious Way* that evening from what we gathered. She was wearing a fur coat and was barefoot. She was a very small woman, thin and under five feet tall. So, in the dark, could be confused for a large animal."

"Oh my God! We had no idea!" She felt an immense crater of guilt crush her.

Warren looked at Alana. "Her son Christopher has issues. He spent some time at the asylum on the mainland back in the 1980s. From what we understand he has been living with his mother Margaret in that home since about 1989. We received some calls that night you hit her, about a man that fits Christopher's description in the road. He was holding something in his arms, screaming in agony. The dead man on the island, who we found shot to death, is Christopher. We believe he is responsible for Spencer and Chelsea's death. What else can you tell me?" he questioned Alana. His pale face peered at her with intensity.

Alana was overwhelmed, she wasn't sure how to react. "I don't know what to say," she replied while she waded through waves of regret.

"What happened when you went to Mirror Island? When did you get there?" the chief asked patiently.

"We arrived on the island on Monday afternoon. Later that evening, Bacon, Derek, and I couldn't find Spencer and Chelsea, so we walked around." She paused as an officer came into the room.

"Hey, Chief, they found a body in the ocean, we gotta go. Think it's the Santiago kid."

"Derek," Alana whispered to herself.

"I gotta go, Alana. We'll talk tomorrow. You can sit with Stacie here. Your parents should be here shortly to get you," he said before hustling out of the police station.

"Derek's body," she said out loud, the words carrying a heavy weight. Alana was numb. Her core was cold, and her sense of life was removed from her body. She felt weightless and lifeless, an empty abyss in an endless sea, much like Mirror Island.

"Jenna was right, she was right all along. We were all doomed from the beginning. We should've listened."

# CHAPTER THIRTEEN

Alana sat in the room and mulled over the information she'd just received. *All of this could have been avoided,* she thought to herself.

A woman walking by outside of the precinct, sobbing, caught her attention. It was Chelsea's mother. She was crying profusely on her husband's shoulder. She saw Alana through the office window, then stormed inside and started screaming in her face.

"You stupid teenagers think you are invincible!"

Alana was mortified and flabbergasted. She wasn't sure how to respond. She threw her hands up to block her face from the spit flying out of this woman's mouth as she yelled at the top of her lungs in pain. Her husband grabbed her as police officers came in and removed Chelsea's mother from the station.

Alana sat there in silence. The vile scene played over in her head. She ran through all the horrific images in her mind.

She wanted to block them out but she couldn't, they were too vivid. Too real.

"I hope they find Bacon alive," she whispered out loud.

As the thought of Brandon being rescued crossed her mind, her mother and father walked in. They were overjoyed to see their daughter and embraced her tightly. They were aware that Spencer and Chelsea had been found brutally murdered and the authorities were still looking for Bacon and Derek.

***

Alana and her family had to stay on Orcas Island for a few days while the police continued their search and investigation. They eventually pulled Derek's body out of the Pacific and searched the island for Bacon but only found his Jansport backpack and red beanie. The search lasted seven days before it was called off and Brandon officially became a missing person.

Alana returned to Tacoma to finish high school and prepare for college at Evergreen State in the fall. While at orientation that summer, she ran into Bacon's older sister Kara, who was going to be a junior at the college that autumn. They exchanged a few words, as well as email addresses. A week after orientation, Alana received an AOL instant messenger chat message from Kara.

*evergreen_kara: Hi Alana!*

*AlanaSk881: Hey Kara! It's so nice to hear from you again.*

*evergreen_kara: It was good running into you at Evergreen State last week. I think you'll love it here; I sure do. If you have any questions or need anything at all, please don't hesitate to reach out. I've been doing a lot of thinking and soul-searching lately. Life seems so different now with my brother missing, but I guess I'm preaching to the choir.*

*AlanaSk881: It was nice to see you too.... Yeah, I'm certainly in the choir. Life seems so different and none of my friends understand. They all treat me like I'm the weird girl now. Like they are waiting for me to snap and go crazy.*

*evergreen_kara: Oh, I'm so sorry to hear that. I can relate. My friends are acting similarly and my boyfriend keeps asking me over and over and over if I'm ok. No, I'm not ok my brother is missing!!*

*AlanaSk881: I miss little Bacon so so much...*

*Evergreen_kara: Me too. I want you to know my brother adored you. He thought you were so awesome and he always told me you were like a second sister to him. That's why I feel confident telling you this. I have to share it with someone and I feel you are the only person who'd understand.*

*AlanaSk881: Tell me what?*

*evergreen_kara: I keep having dreams that Brandon is alive. They're incredibly real and raw. He's in this dimly lit room and he looks different. His hair is short and he looks even skinnier. I mean, he was always thin, but this is sickly. He's asking for my help and each time when I go to hug him, I wake up crying. There's a part of me that can't help but think he's still alive on the island. I know that sounds crazy cause it's been a few months, but the dreams are so real. I'm so sorry to dump this on you. I know you've been through a lot. I just don't know who to talk to.*

*AlanaSk881: Weird!!!!!!!!!!!!!!! I've been having similar dreams. He's in a dark room, has super short hair, and looks like he's starving.*

*evergreen_kara: WHAT!!!!!!!!!!!!!!!!! FOR REAL??!!*

*AlanaSk881: For real. I'm not kidding. That's so crazy. What the fuck do you think it means? Do you think he's alive?*

*Evergreen_kara: So crazy! Hey, my boyfriend's home. Talk later. PS: I'm going to be in town this weekend if you're around.*

Alana felt a strong sense of fear overtake her. Her knees shook and she tried to process the conversation. She felt nauseous and dizzy. "No way, no fucking way," she murmured to herself.

Alana was dumbfounded. She was having the same dream as Kara. Ever since she returned to the mainland, she'd been having recurring dreams weekly that Bacon was alive. He was in a dark room, his hair was cut short, and he was emaciated. She originally shrugged them off as a product of her trauma, however, now she felt they were a sign.

"If Lewis has been living there for twenty years, then it's possible Bacon is alive. Maybe he fell down a ravine or went unconscious due to being so fucked up. Maybe Lewis found him and has been nursing him back to health," she said to herself.

The thought reminded her of Lewis and how he took such great care of her. She was forever grateful for his kind-hearted nature and the fact he saved her life. If it wasn't for him, Alana would certainly be dead. Christopher would've choked her to death as he did to her friends. She was certain of it.

A few more days passed and the weekend approached. It was a sunny late July, Saturday afternoon when Alana got another direct message from Kara.

*evergreen_kara: Hey Alana! I'm at my rent's house! Do you wanna meet up tonight? I'd love to talk more. My boyfriend Grant is with me if that's ok.*

*AlanaSk881: Hey Kara. Yeah, that's cool. Where do you want to meet up?*

*evergreen_kara: I'm house-sitting for my parents, come over! Just Grant and I here and the animals. Come by at 8.*

*AlanaSk881: Cool. Sounds like a plan. C ya then.*

\*\*\*

Eight o'clock approached and Alana took a walk over to the Bacon residence, a short hike through some side streets. It was a warm summer evening and the frogs and cicadas serenaded the sun as it descended. A crescent moon began its ascension as she approached the front door and knocked firmly. Inside, dogs barked and she saw a blurry figure coming to the door through the stained glass windows beside it.

"Hey!" Kara said as she put her arms around Alana.

They hugged for a few moments. They were both very happy to see each other considering what they'd been through. Alana was quiet and nervous.

"C'mon in," Kara said, waving toward the living room.

"I feel like I haven't been here in years," Alana replied, her heart fluttering in her chest. She was overwhelmed. She was not expecting to feel this emotion right away but she'd spent a lot of time at their house growing up, hanging out with her crew in the basement.

"How long has it been?" Kara asked, putting her bleached hair in a bun.

"Like a few months, but it seems longer," Alana answered with a laugh.

Kara chuckled too. "This is my boyfriend Grant. He's a junior at Evergreen, as well. He plays on the baseball team."

"Hey, Alana, nice to meet you," he said. He was tall and burly. He looked intimidating but genuine.

"Hi," Alana mumbled in response.

She was feeling anxious and insecure being there. The whole situation was becoming intense and she was beginning to think it was a bad idea to come over.

She wasn't sure she was ready to see pictures of Bacon. They were everywhere. His family had gone through all of their photo albums and pulled every picture from the dust and taped them to the walls, to the fridge, everywhere. The photos decorated the entire home. They were grieving and they had every right to. They had no answers and no idea where their family member was. Kara shifted around the living room before heading into the kitchen and opening the fridge.

"Do you want anything to drink? We got like every damn soda, wine, beer if you want it?" she asked Alana.

"I'll take a cream soda," she replied, certain there were dozens in the fridge. Their family loved cream soda and the house was usually full of boxes of it.

"You know us too well," Kara admitted with a giggle.

Grant was quiet as the two young ladies spoke about Bacon and discussed their sorrow.

"So, you are having a similar dream?" Kara asked, her eyes filled with desperation.

"Yeah, almost sounds identical. I'm all of a sudden in this dungeon-like room, I can see fire light flickering on the walls. It's dim and I'm lost and confused. Then, all of a sudden, I see Bacon. He's extremely thin and he looks ill. His eyes are sunken in and he has deep, rigid bags under them. His hair is really short. He looks terrified, then he asks me for my help. That's when I wake up every time."

Kara's eyes widened and she took a moment to process what Alana told her. "That's exactly what my dream is like. Do you think it's possible my brother is still alive on that island or is that completely insane to think? Why else would we both be having the same dream?"

Alana mulled over her experience with Lewis in her head. She was unsure if she should tell Kara about him. At the same time, she thought maybe Bacon was alive and eventually found Lewis. However, she knew with his kindhearted nature, Lewis certainly would have traveled to the mainland and at least dumped Brandon off to be discovered. Something wasn't right.

Despite his desire to be isolated and left alone in solitude, she thought there was no way he'd sacrifice her friend's life for his own selfish needs. That was not the Lewis she'd met. She decided to tell Alana and Grant the part of the story she'd left out when she spoke to the police. When asked who shot Christopher in the back and saved her life, Alana told them that a hunter on the island shot him to death before fleeing off the island by boat.

The police had been searching for a man that didn't exist. Alana sat back in the recliner and panned her eyes over the fireplace mantle at the pictures of Bacon. They were lined up in various heights and sizes. There were images of him playing baseball and basketball as a little kid. There were several pictures of him and his siblings hiking or camping.

One picture in particular caught her attention. It was one of Brandon high up in a fir tree. He looked to be about thirteen and he'd climbed up into the branches, looking very proud of himself.

He had a giant grin from ear to ear, making her heart break all over again.

"Well... there is a possibility he could be alive. There's a part of the story I haven't told anyone, including my parents or the police. If I tell you, you have to both promise me this won't leave this house. You have to give me your absolute word. Promise me," she said, her voice dead serious.

"Of course. Promise," Kara replied with hesitation.

"Promise," Grant said as he motioned with his hands that his mouth was zipped shut.

"You guys know the story of Lewis Ford?"

"The kid that went missing back in the day on Mirror Island?" Grant inquired.

"Yeah, back in the seventies, right?" Kara commented.

"Yeah. Well, he's alive and he's been living on Mirror Island for twenty years. He's the one who shot the killer, not a hunter. He saved my life. I vowed to him that I'd keep his life on the island a secret, so I made up a story about a rogue hunter. He's a very sweet man. He even has a dog and a kitty he takes care of that someone dumped on the island. If Bacon is alive, it's possible he found Lewis."

"Are you serious? Do you think he'd help Brandon get to the mainland?" Kara questioned.

"I'd think so, he does value his secrecy. Maybe Bacon and him are on the island together?" Alana said.

"What? You're kidding me?" Kara exclaimed in astonishment.

"Your fucking with us, right?" Grant asked.

"I wouldn't do that, not after what I've been through, as well as Kara's family."

"That's not Alana's style," Kara responded swiftly.

"We should go out there and look," Grant suggested, scratching his goatee. His scraggly, unkempt hair hung over his eyes as he brushed the strands out of his face.

"I don't want to put Alana through that after what she's been through already," Kara contested.

"It's ok. I'll go," Alana insisted.

Kara perked up. "Are you sure?"

"Yeah. After all, that piece of shit is dead, so I feel okay going back out there. Anything for Bacon," Alana confessed.

# Chapter Fourteen

"**W**ill Lewis be pissed if he finds out you told us about him?" Grant asked.

"I think, given the circumstances, he might not be. I mean Lewis and Bacon would probably get along, so if he did survive and Lewis found him, it's possible Bacon convinced him to let him stay there on the island."

"Yeah, but there's no weed on Mirror Island," Kara said and winked.

Everyone laughed and discussed a plan of action for going to the island. Alana sat there, digesting everything. The reality was maybe Bacon had survived and in his state of despair, decided he wanted to stay on the island. He was an odd one after all, adventurous and outdoorsy. The idea that he was alive and flourishing with Lewis made Alana feel a sense of joy, something she hadn't felt since before the trip to the island.

Mirror Island in its elusive lore was enchanting like some powerful and ancient elixir. It was as if the land existed as its own separate living and breathing entity that was lonely, desperately drawing people into its grasp.

"Have you ever been, Grant? We went once in high school," Kara told them.

"I went once in eighth grade, as well, with my dad on a hiking trip. We took the trail to the overlook, that was about it. But if we're going, we gotta go armed and prepared. I have a hunting rifle with a scope I'll bring."

"Please, we need to be prepped for any and everything on that island. I don't think I can stay the night, though, if I'm being honest," Alana admitted.

The idea of sleeping on the island scared her. She felt safe and secure with Christopher dead, but she still had a lot to process and wasn't sure she might ever be able to sleep or camp on the island again. Or any other island, for that matter.

"What are you going to tell your parents?" Grant inquired.

"Tell them you're going to be at Evergreen with me at my apartment, so you can check the school and area out more," Kara suggested.

"Ok, that might work," Alana responded with uncertainty. She hated the idea of lying to her parents again. but she felt this was the only chance Kara and her family might have at closure. The search had been called off after a week due to heavy rains and inclement weather. It'd already been delayed due to fog and severe thunderstorms, so her family couldn't help but feel a lackluster effort was made by the search and rescue crew.

"When should we go?" Kara asked. "The sooner, the better."

"This weekend is perfect," Grant suggested, reaching for the remote and flipping through the TV channels. He landed on an X-Files rerun.

"Oh, this is a good one. Mulder breaks out of the Siberian prison!" he mentioned with a hoot.

Kara felt hopeful. "Does that work for you, Alana?"

"Sure."

"Saturday it is!" Grant shouted.

"Are you sure you're ok with this?" Kara persisted.

"I think it's the only way to get some closure," Alana replied in a faint whisper.

"Me too," Kara muttered in agreement.

The evening ended and Alana headed home right before midnight. The week flew by, before she knew it was Friday and she was preparing for her trip to Mirror Island. She followed Kara's lead, telling her parents she'd be at Evergreen State for the weekend with Kara. Despite everything, they didn't think twice and insisted she go have a fun relaxing weekend in Olympia.

Kara and Grant picked her up in his forest green Four-Runner and they headed to Orcas Island. It was rainy and foggy when they arrived. They checked into a motel with two beds and talked about their plans to head to Mirror Island early the next morning.

Nightfall came and Alana and Kara both had the same dream about Bacon, but this time they each said he told them to *hurry*.

They considered the severity of the dream and decided they'd head out right before sunrise, so they could arrive on the island at dawn. In the early morning darkness, the trio headed to the marina to get Grant's boat moored there. A blanket of fog fluttered over the dark waters as mist rose and met the cool morning air. Alana, Kara, and Grant boarded the runabout and sailed off to Mirror Island. Light rain fell from above as clouds and fog intermingled with each other. The boat cruised through the placid water, creating ripples behind it.

The island was hidden in the quilt of fog that hung over the terrain like a lingering phantom. The craggy overlook was buried in the clouds. A shadow of evergreens stretched through the fog, making their presence known. The landscape appeared rough and rigid. As it lay hidden beneath the morning gloom, a rush of dismay overcame Alana.

Through the fog, she was reliving the night of the accidents and the horrific events that transpired shortly thereafter. She could hear her friend Jenna's voice whispering along the wind as it blew over the sea. Dread trickled in as she tried to shove the feeling aside and focus on the task at hand. In the end, the man who was after them was dead. All that remained ahead was a looming mass of ancient wilderness.

"It looks so majestic standing out of the ocean and immense fog like that," Grant yelled over the sound of the engine.

"It's sort of eerie and haunting," Kara replied.

Alana stood silent as they approached the dock and the motor seized. The very dock where she found Derek dead before he was dumped in the Pacific by Christopher. She knew the biggest fear would be not finding any sign of Bacon, or worse, finding his dead body. If they discovered his corpse, though, she thought it might at least bring his family some closure.

Rainfall began to accelerate as they started their journey into the woods. They all three walked quietly as they shifted from a driftwood-riddled beach to a dense forest thicket. Wandering for the better part of an hour, they paused by some cedar trees to eat ham and cheese sandwiches with salt and vinegar potato chips. The crunch of the crisps was reminiscent of leaves in autumn, the crackling reminding Alana of stepping on bones near the altar. She replayed the memory of discovering the moss-covered corpse like a film in her head.

"I think I remember how to get us at least near where Lewis frequently goes. Maybe we can find him there. Who knows, maybe Bacon is living the high life," Alana told them.

"Perfect. We'll follow you," Kara replied.

"I'm so glad I brought this rifle. These woods are giving me the creeps," Grant noted, clenching the weapon and tightening his grip.

"It's only trees, ferns, and forest debris," Kara stated, observing the evergreens that surrounded them.

"Yeah, but it's what lurks beneath it all in the darkness and shadows that scares me," Grant murmured.

"What are you scared of? Lewis Ford?" Kara asked with a sarcastic grin.

Alana interjected, "Lewis is a sweetheart."

"Sounds like it. He saved your life and he rescues abandoned pups and kitties. Sounds like an angel if you ask me," Kara chimed in.

Grant gazed at the shadows sitting before them at the darkest edges of the forest and spoke, "Even angels fall, Kara."

They descended into a lower part of the island. It was near the inlet, a part of the terrain where a river ran through a crevice, creating a crack in the island. Steep, serrated cliffs loomed over the rugged stone faces into the frigid, opaque water below. The group looked up at the sharp incline that erected out of the cold earth as they maneuvered near the drop-off to the river.

"We need to cut around this way. That will lead us inward further into the forest and to the center of the island," Alana suggested.

Giant firs and evergreens lined the pathway into the wilderness. With each step, the woods got thicker and thicker.

Alana circled the area, searching for a landmark. "There's a path around here somewhere. I know there is. It's one of Lewis's hidden footpaths. It's by a giant boulder that looks like a bear. Follow me this way."

"A bear eh?" Grant muttered grimly, his eyes lifted to the sky.

"Yeah, you hike through these dense evergreens, then there's this boulder that looks like a bear silhouette walking. There are a few other small rock faces near it, but this one is recognizable. Then, right past it, is a small meadow with ferns and creepy doll heads," Alana stated.

"Creepy doll heads!" Kara and Grant both exclaimed.

Grant appeared mortified. "You didn't tell us about the creepy doll heads!"

"It's nothing to worry about. It's how Lewis keeps people away from the areas he uses regularly," Alana answered.

"Nice choice of horror, I like it," Kara giggled.

"There it is!" Alana shouted.

"Where? Let me see!" Grant exclaimed, rushing in front of both women.

"It does look like a bear," Kara said as she gazed at the rock protruding from the ground.

"That's a big, random boulder in this forest. Maybe because there are no bears here on the island, nature was like here... here is a bear, Mirror Island," Grant announced to the forest.

"You're weird," Kara replied, her eyes fixed on the craggy, grey boulder.

All of a sudden, they heard the faint sounds of screaming.

"Did you guys hear that?" Alana inquired.

"Yeah, I hear screaming off in the distance, further ahead," Grant answered quickly. He held the gun and peered around the greenwood.

"Listen," Alana whispered. The screams continued. "They're coming from over here!"

# Chapter Fifteen

The trio ventured further into the desolate landscapes and closer to the howls ahead of them. Once they got near, both Kara and Alana recognized the screams. They were from Bacon.

"That sounds like Brandon," Kara whispered. Her breath quivered with trepidation.

"That's Bacon," Alana insisted without a doubt.

"He must be hurt or trapped somewhere. Maybe a boulder pinned him or something," Grant suggested.

They listened attentively to ensure they went in the right direction. When they got closer, Alana recognized where they were. Soon, they'd be approaching the various altars and the unnamed corpse. Bacon's screams were getting louder and more desperate. With each step they took, his yells increased in volume. That's when they saw him. The scene was terrifying.

Alana and Kara shrieked as they ran to him. He was frail and malnourished. His eyes and cheeks were sunken and his face was chiseled and gaunt like the steep slopes of the cliffs of Mirror Island. He was naked and his hair was cut short. It was choppy and uneven. He could barely speak as they approached him. He lay lifeless in a rusty metal cage, shaking profusely. There was no one around, the steel box sat alone in the middle of the desolate meadow.

"We need to get him out of there, now!" Kara exclaimed.

"Watch out!" Grant hollered.

He ran over to the cage and pulled out a small hammer from his pack. He began smashing the lock until it busted open.

"I knew this tool bag would come in handy," he said.

Alana opened the cage and Grant pulled Bacon out of it. He was skin and bones, on death's door. He couldn't speak, but he was breathing.

"Who put you in that?" Kara asked in a panic.

Bacon tried to muster up the energy to speak but he couldn't. Alana panned around the woods line and spotted the altar entrance. She ran over to it and was met by the string of severed doll heads and animal bone totems.

"What the fuck?" she cried out in horror.

"Alana, what?" Kara asked as she approached the altar with Grant by her side.

"Creepy," Grant mumbled in agreement.

"These doll heads were bald last time I was here," Alana stuttered.

"Bald?" Kara replied.

Alana stood before the altar with the line of totems and examined the hair on their heads. There were over thirty doll heads painted with black ink around the eyes. They were covered in brown hair that appeared to have been glued on.

Kara began to shake when she realized it was her brother's hair. Just then, they heard a man yell. They turned to see Lewis approaching them. Grant placed Brandon on the forest floor and reached for his rifle, aiming it at Lewis's chest.

"What are you doing, you idiots?" Lewis demanded.

"Lewis, did you do this to Brandon?" Alana asked with fear, her eyes scanning his every move.

"No. It wasn't me. It was her," he answered.

"Her, who is she?" Alana asked.

"Mother Nature," Lewis whispered.

"I don't understand. Lewis, please, did you put him in there?" Alana asked again.

"Goddamn it, you fucking child! I told you, I didn't put the son of a bitch in the cell! She did it. It was her!" he howled.

Lewis pointed to a dead fir tree. It was about ten feet high. It stood straight up, then splintered at the top to the left and right, creating a set of crooked antlers.

Resembling a totem pole in its own regard, it was a light gray with cracks running down either side of it. They were faint and spread lightly throughout the deadwood. At the base of the tree was an altar of animal bones and decaying flesh. The animal was unrecognizable as maggots and flies covered the decomposing corpse.

Alana realized they were standing near the skeleton covered in moss and lichen. She gazed past Lewis and could see the altar with the corpse covered in forest debris below it.

Alana was petrified. Her body froze as she processed her environment.

"Lewis, what's going on? Why are you doing this?"

Grant stood with the rifle raised. Lewis held a shotgun in his hand as he got closer to them.

"Take one more step and I'll fucking shoot!" Grant dictated as he raised the weapon.

Lewis aimed his shotgun at Grant and spoke, "You don't understand. She gives and she takes. And it is time we make a final offering to the island."

"He's fucking lost it," Grant insisted with his focus on Lewis, who was pacing back and forth.

"Please, he's my brother!" Kara cried out.

"That's exactly why he must go. It's his time, she has decided. We've been preparing for the sacrifice for months. I've been prepping your brother for his sacrament. Just like I offered twenty years ago," he proclaimed, nodding his head toward the skeleton covered in moss and lichen beneath the altar.

"You told me you found him like that?" Alana whispered, the horror of reality washing over her.

"That is true. When I found William he was on death's door. He'd come here to Mirror Island, much like I had. But when I discovered him, it was too late. He'd been out here for years and the isolation got the best of him. He begged me to bring him to the mainland to see a doctor. He believed he was ill. But he wasn't sick, he was infected and he needed to be sacrificed. The island is hungry... for children, for men... it feeds. It devours the weak and vulnerable men. Men like myself," he explained.

Both guys kept their weapons pointed at each other as silence fell over the muted landscape. Lewis began to shake and tremble. His eyes were fluttering back and forth in his head. He stood for a moment, wobbling left and right. The shotgun swayed in the afternoon air. His eyes convulsed and Lewis started screaming at the top of his lungs.

He dropped the shotgun and began thrashing around on the ground, chanting, "Eat the flesh, there's nothing left. Eat the flesh, there's nothing left."

Over and over he chanted it as loud as he could. His fists plummeted toward the ground as he punched and sang, "Eat the flesh, there's nothing left. Eat the flesh, there's nothing left."

He rose and ran over to the deceased fir tree, collapsing in front of it. He continued to belt out the repeating phrase. Lewis raised his hands to his head and started yanking out clumps of his tangled hair, then eating it. He screamed louder and louder.

> *"Eat the flesh, there's nothing left,*
> *eat the flesh, there's nothing left,*
> *eat the flesh, there's nothing left,*
> *eat the flesh, there's nothing left,*
> *eat the flesh, there's nothing left,*
> *eat the flesh, there's nothing left."*

Then, the rhyme scheme changed.

> *"Build the nest, and lay to rest,*
> *build the nest, and lay to rest,*

*build the nest, and lay to rest,*
*build the nest, and lay to rest,*
*build the nest, and lay to rest,*
*build the nest, and lay to rest,*
*build the nest, and lay to rest,*
*build the nest, and lay to rest,*
*build the nest, and lay to rest,*
*build the nest, and lay to rest,*
*build the nest, and lay to rest,*
*build the nest, and lay to rest."*

Over and over he chanted, ripping all the hair from his head. Lewis clenched clumps of gray strands in his hands and cried out,

*"Build the nest, and lay to rest,*
*build the nest, and lay to rest,*
*eat the flesh, there's nothing left,*
*eat the flesh, there's nothing left,*
*build the nest, and lay to rest,*
*build the nest, and lay to rest,*
*eat the flesh, there's nothing left,*
*eat the flesh, there's nothing left,*
*build the nest, and lay to rest,*
*build the nest, and lay to rest."*

# CHAPTER SIXTEEN

Lewis's father was abusive. He'd continuously beat his son when he'd drink. Lewis's mother passed away when he was a young teen and he was left with his demonic father, fending for himself. With the loss of his mother, his dad took everything out on Lewis and beat him violently.

Eventually, the abuse took its toll on the boy and he fled to Mirror Island to start a new life for himself. When he arrived, he thought he was alone. He'd learn after a few months, he wasn't the only person there on the island. He stumbled upon an old man who'd left to live away from society and was now reaching the end of his life. The old man was ill and in desperate need of medical attention, care that could save his life. The man had contracted an infection and was approaching death.

Lewis could've taken the man to the mainland to see a doctor, but he chose not to. Instead, he sat with the man while he suffered and passed away. Lewis didn't know why he didn't help the man, but something in him resisted.

*** 

Lewis continued to convulse and shake on the ground before crawling to his feet and staggering toward Alana in a daze.

"He seems hypnotized," Grant commented, his voice low and wary.

Lewis opened his eyes and spoke, "I haven't been honest with you, Alana. I'm not as I seem. I've been kidnapping people and bringing them to Mirror Island for years. I cut off all their hair and slowly eat it while I starve them. Right before they reach death's door, I summon a spirit and feed them to her.

Just then, a ring in the distance caught their attention. It was loud and piercing. The noise reverberated throughout the island. Everyone plummeted to their knees as they watched a woman in a black dress materialize in the middle of the forest. Her face was muted and scathed, her skin weathered and gray. Her hair was made of dead leaves and deserted bird nests.

"Mother!" Lewis called out.

The ring intensified as the students trembled before fainting to the ground in a trance.

When they awoke, they were chained in a dark, dilapidated cabin. Grant turned to his side to find Alana and Kara bound on the other side of the dimly lit room. The door to the cabin swung open and Lewis stepped inside. He was in a hood and ritual gear.

He stood there quietly as the sound of the spirit moving through the vast Washington wilderness serenaded the jagged outcroppings of Mirror Island. The trio observed the shadowy figure as she made her way toward them. The ringing of a bell around her neck grew in volume and echoed out above the barren landscapes. It was melodic, yet haunting. With each step she took, the bell became louder and louder. The entity began to sing.

*"Oh dark one, oh dark one, oh darkest of sons, offer me your flesh, please take only one."*
*"Oh dark one, oh dark one, oh darkest of sons, offer me your flesh, please take only one."*
*"Oh dark one, oh dark one, oh darkest of sons, offer me your flesh, please take only one."*

Lewis removed all three of them from the cabin, dragging them into the blackness lingering in the wild. The moon hung above, giving life to the night sky. Alana gazed up and stared at the stars.

"I guess I'll be joining you soon," she said to herself.

"Please, don't kill us," Kara demanded. She looked beside her to see Brandon lying in the rusty cage. He was emaciated to the point of starvation.

"You're going to hell!" Grant screamed.

"I'm already there," Lewis replied flatly.

"Lewis, I know you have love in your heart. I saw it. The way you love for your animals," Alana told him. Her eyes were fixated on Lewis's every move.

"Mother, take them to The Dark One!" Lewis commanded.

The woman in the black dress glided toward the students in chains. She wielded a handmade wooden spear in her withered hand. It was beautifully crafted, ancient, and primordial like the branches of the evergreens adorning Mirror Island.

In one swift motion, she lifted the spear in the air and shoved it into Grant's stomach. Kara and Alana tried to scream but they were paralyzed. The blood trickled out onto the pine needles and Lewis scurried over to his corpse and started devouring Grant's flesh.

The teen's throat gurgled and his body convulsed violently as the ghostly figure kissed Lewis delicately on his head before gathering Grant's remains and throwing them on the giant altar. Together, Lewis and the spirit in the black dress sang loudly.

> *"Oh dark one, oh dark one, oh darkest of sons, offer me your flesh, please take only one."*
> *"Oh dark one, oh dark one, oh darkest of sons, offer me your flesh, please take only one."*
> *"Oh dark one, oh dark one, oh darkest of sons, offer me your flesh, please take only one."*

"I have brought you another, will you please love me, Mother?" Lewis asked the mirage. The being's hair turned to serpents. They were gray and hissing, baring their fangs at Lewis.

"That is not enough, my child, bring me another. Bring me the others," she demanded.

Lewis went over to the cage and retrieved Bacon's slender frame.

"He is nothing but skin and bones, he barely counts for one," she told him. Brandon looked diseased and unconscious. Lewis grabbed Kara and brought her closer to the spirit.

"Here's another, his sister, surely this shall count as one," he whispered gently.

"Eat him, feed me her."

"Of course, Mother." Lewis followed her lead. He dragged Kara closer to the woman in the black dress. Her face was unclear and distorted. The sound of the bell around her neck reverberated through the wild.

"Here, kill him," the spirit dictated while handing Lewis the well-sharpened spear. "You know what to do with it," she insisted.

Without hesitation, Lewis lifted the stake high into the sky and rammed it into Bacon's beating heart. Kara and Alana watched in terror, unable to scream. Something was preventing their bodies from moving or speaking.

Bacon's frail remains sat beneath the spear lifeless. His corpse resembled a mangled hotdog stuck between a toothpick on a cracker at a horrific dinner party.

"Perfect," the spirit said as she glided across the forest floor.

"I love you, Mother," Lewis told her.

"I love you, too, child. Now eat, my son."

Lewis fell to the ground and began digging his teeth into Bacon's skin, ripping bits of his flesh with each violent tear. The sound of his intestines being torn by Lewis's teeth was unsettling. The man continued to devour bits of Brandon's insides, chewing on parts of his spleen. Bits of entrails hung from Lewis's blood-stained teeth.

"Good boy, Lewis," the woman said softly.

"Your turn, Mother."

The woman in the black dress raised the spear and stabbed Kara repeatedly. Her body flailed as the weapon entered her heart and killed her.

When she was done with Kara, the spirit hovered over Alana. She knelt beside her and whispered, "You should not have returned. No one escapes Mirror Island a second time. He let you go, yet you came back. That was foolish."

Alana tried to speak but her body was numb, she couldn't move a muscle. The entity held her ghostly hands over Alana's heart and began to sing.

"Awaken my daughter, awaken your spirit. Bring me your demons and allow me to own your soul. Awaken my daughter and open your eyes, for you are the daughter I have been waiting for. Your life is now mine."

Without hesitation, the spirit shifted into Alana's body. She blinked her eyes and looked around, taking in her new body. She examined her extremities and smiled.

"Mother, you have a body again!" Lewis cried out.

"Yes, my child. Now let's go home."

# ACKNOWLEDGMENTS

Thank you to my editor and publisher, Juliet Rose, for helping make this story the best it could be. Thank you also to Kirsten Noelle Craig for taking the time to read it and provide feedback. You are the best! Thank you to the readers. Without you, none of this would be possible!

*Check out my other work at:*

abovetheraincollective.com

*Books:*

The Nomad (novella 2024)
Final Passenger (anthology, 2024)